BY PATRICIA BEATTY

Be Ever Hopeful, Hannalee

Bonanza Girl

Charley Skedaddle

The Coach That Never Came

Eight Mules from Monterey

Lupita Mañana

O the Red Rose Tree

The Nickel-Plated Beauty

Sarah and Me and the Lady from the Sea

Turn Homeward, Hannalee

Wait for Me, Watch For Me, Eula Bee

Who Comes with Cannons?

TURN

HOMEWARD,

HANNALEE

PATRICIA
BEATTY

A BEECH TREE PAPERBACK BOOK
NEW YORK

www.williammorrow.com
Printed in the United States of America

The Library of Congress has cataloged the Morrow Junior Books
edition of *Turn Homeward, Hannalee* as follows:
Beatty, Patricia. Turn homeward, Hannalee.
Summary: Twelve-year-old Hannalee Reed, forced to relocate in
Indiana along with other Georgia millworkers during the Civil War,
leaves her mother with a promise to return home as soon as the war
ends. ISBN 0-688-03871-9
[1. United States—History—Civil War, 1861–1865—Fiction.
2. Georgia—History—Fiction. 3. Textile workers—Fiction.
4. Children—Employment—Fiction.] I. Title.
PZ7.B380544Tu 1984 [Fic] 84-8960

        7 9 10 8
First Beech Tree Edition, 1999
ISBN 0-688-16676-8

For Jessie Pauline Robbins, my mother

Contents

TURN
HOMEWARD,
HANNALEE

Chapter One

The Scarlet Skies

I T WAS THE CRYING FROM DOWN BELOW THAT WOKE ME up that hot night. I caught the words clear as the mill bell: "No, you can't say that to me. You can't say you won't two times, Davey Reed, not again you can't!"

I sat up to listen, being careful not to pull on the bedclothes and disturb Mama, who was asleep beside me.

Then I heard another, deeper voice, saying something softly. After that came a wordless cry, then a wild weeping, and a minute later the sound of somebody running.

Rosellen! It was Rosellen and my older brother, Davey, down there talking at the front door. No, not talking—quarreling. Rosellen was the one who did most of the talking and then ran off. It must have been a really fierce quarrel for her to raise her voice. That wasn't like Rosellen Sanders.

I sighed, listening now to hear if Mama had been woken up, too; but no, her breathing hadn't changed. Mama had slept through the ruckus below our window. That was good. With the baby coming, she needed her rest these days. I lay back on my pillow and closed my eyes, hoping to fall asleep fast, but I knew I wouldn't. I used to sleep like a log, but since the war had begun three years ago, every time I woke up at night I stayed awake for a long time. I'd lie awake worrying about Davey, who is fighting in the Confederate Army, and about us Reeds, now that Pap died in an army hospital last winter. And now I had a new worry—the misery between Davey and his longtime true love, Rosellen.

While I was pondering them, I heard Mama stir. Then I heard her say, "Hannalee, do I hear you sighin'?"

"Yes, Mama, I was. I'm not asleep. Do you want somethin'?"

It was her turn to sigh into the dark. She whispered, "Honey, would you fetch me some cold water? Not from the pitcher in the pantry but from the pump outside. I'd like some real cold well water. I'm dry as an old bone from all that talkin' tonight with you and Davey and the Sanderses. I'm hot, and the baby's movin' in me. He's woke up, too."

I swung my legs over the side of the bed and stayed there for a minute, thinking of the baby that was to come in the fall. Mama always spoke of the baby as "him." I hoped this baby would be a boy, and favor Pap in being redheaded. None of the rest of us, neither Davey, my little ten-year-old brother, Jem, nor I, had his hair. We were all black-haired and brown-eyed, and favored Mama, who had some Cherokee Indian blood in her family. Pap's dying was a deep ache to us, and a boy baby who looked like him would be a comfort.

I found the chinaware cup on the pine table next to the bed on my side, picked it up, and made my way across the room and down the stairs as quietly as I could. I didn't want to wake up Jem as I went past his bedroom.

I walked through the dark house and went outside into the hot night. It was late June, and the red rambler rose that Pap had planted beside the back door was in bloom. He'd planted the sweet-smelling rose even though this wasn't really our house but one we rented from the millowners. But that had been like Pap—he had always favored pretty things.

Thinking of him, I looked up at the sky. That was when I saw it—the bright red flare to the southwest. I pressed the cup to my chest, watching. There it was again! Another blaze of red, and then another. They were sharp bursts of light that came and went, always in the southwest. I knew they weren't summer lightning. Lightning made jagged streaks slicing through the sky or sometimes sheets of light that lit up everything. Besides, lightning was white or blue, not red, and thunder came after it. These flashes were silent, like suddenly blossoming red flowers.

I didn't like them. A cold little breeze that went right through my old cotton nightgown made me shiver. Fear caught hold of me, the same kind that now came to me whenever I met up with anything strange. Pap's dying of camp fever in Virginia had done that to me. Mama confessed she felt the same way, too, now that he was gone from us.

While I watched the red lights, I suddenly heard a soft coughing from somewhere near me. When it came again, I knew who it was. Davey. He'd come around from the front of the house. Davey'd brought a cough back home with him from his army camp in Virginia. He'd been sick like Pap, but he'd gotten over it except for the cough. He'd come home on furlough for a week and was going back to Virginia the day after tomorrow.

Before I could call out his name, he asked fiercely, "Who's out here? I can hear you breathin'."

"Me, Hannalee. I'm goin' to get some cold water for Mama. Did you think I was a Yankee boy, Davey?"

"Bein' a soldier makes a man careful . . ." He shut off what he had meant to say and told me, "Get the water and get inside, little sister. You shouldn't be walkin' around in the dark."

"I won't be long at the pump. Davey, what's that over there in the sky to the south and west? Can you see the red lights?"

"Uh-huh, I been lookin' at 'em for some time now." After a moment he said, "That's artillery, cannons firin'. They're too far off to be heard, but you can see the fire of 'em in the night. It's the war come back here again. That's the way it was in May at Resaca and last fall at Chickamauga. If you'd been outside then, you could'a seen the cannons at Resaca at night, too."

I told him, "I reckon I didn't go out those times at night. Are they our cannons, Davey?"

"I dunno. Some probably have to be Confederate. Cannons firin' means soldiers fightin'. Nobody shoots off cannons for nothin'."

"Where are they?"

"I can't say for certain. Like I told you, they're too far away to be heard, but you can see their fire for miles and miles. I reckon they're somewhere in the mountains southwest of us, and that sure does put them in Georgia!" Davey let out his breath. "We'll know tomorrow night, when Howell comes to get me to go back to Virginia with him. He lives west of here."

I came up to Davey and grabbed him by one arm, saying, "Will the bluebelly Yankees come here to Roswell after you leave again? When they were at Resaca, the folks who owned the mill here moved to Savannah to keep themselves safe. That worries us, Davey."

"Now, don't you fret over that. I can tell you that that smart-as-paint Gen'ral Joe Johnston'll put himself and plenty of Confederate troops between you and any Yankees who have it in mind to come deeper into Georgia. That shootin's a fair distance off. You get the water and get up to bed. You got to go to the mill tomorrow and work like always."

"I didn't forget that, Davey. I never do." I was trying to make the time with him last as long as I could. Since he'd come home, I hadn't had any time alone with him. He'd comforted Mama and told her, yes, to name the baby Paul after Pap; he'd talked to Jem about Gettysburg and the battles he'd been in; but most of all he'd been off courting with Rosellen. There hadn't been any time for me at all. I wasn't sure he even knew how much I valued him because he was my brother and because he was a brave soldier of the Confederate Army.

I still held on to Davey, but I couldn't think of the things I'd been storing up to say to him. There were too many of them, and the few minutes I had with him now had come about by accident. I said finally, "Davey, I couldn't help but hear you and Rosellen carryin' on under my window. I wasn't listenin' in on purpose, but I heard her yell at you, and then I heard her weepin' and runnin' off. What's the trouble?"

He grunted. "She says I am. Rosellen wanted me to marry up with her b'fore I left. She pressed me hard as thunder to tie the knot. She said she'd got the preacher primed and ready and has her ma's gold ring and all. I care for Rosellen. By all the Holy Hokies, I come constant to her. Someday I'll marry with her, but not now. I won't come back to her in a nailed-down wooden box because I got killed in some battle. I said no to marryin' her when

I was furloughed home last time, and I said it again this time, too. It's enough that Pap came back in a wood box. If I get killed, it'd rest easier on my heart to leave her a grievin' sweetheart than a widow like Ma. But she don't see it that way. She had it in mind to be Mrs. Sergeant Davey Reed, and she's plenty put out with me. She wouldn't even let me walk her home."

As I stared at the red bursts of light, I pondered Rosellen and what Davey had just told me about her. I truly admired Rosellen Sanders and had looked forward to her becoming part of the family. She was just about the best drawing girl in the whole cloth mill where Jem and I worked, too. Rosellen was beautiful, gold-fair, gray-eyed, and slimly straight as a willow branch—"all over beautiful," as everybody said. Lots of other mill girls were jealous of her beauty and said spiteful things to and about her, but she only tossed her head and laughed in their faces. She was as headstrong and smart as she was handsome. So far as I knew, nobody but Davey had ever stood up to her and told her no, and he'd done it two times.

I sighed as I let go of my brother's arm. He wasn't in any temper to talk with me about anything, not even the reading and writing lessons I'd just started with the new preacher's wife. When I learned how, I'd be the only Reed who could read and write.

I left him and went to the pump to draw up a cup of cold water for Mama. As I worked the handle, I thought about Rosellen. Maybe, in spite of what had happened between her and Davey, I could talk to her at the mill and get her to come to Davey's farewell dinner. Maybe I could help out somehow. Her Aunt Marilla and Mama and Pap had been friends so long as I could remember. I knew Rosellen better than I knew just about anybody else in town.

Davey was still at the back door. As I came near him, I could smell our homemade ash and lye soap on his clothing stronger than I could the scent of the roses. He told me, "Hannalee, I wish I didn't have to go back to Virginia with the baby comin'. I wish the war was over and done with."

I couldn't help asking what had been on my mind lots of times. "Why is the state of Virginia more important than Georgia, so that you have to leave us and go back up there?"

He flared at me. "You asked me that same thing last time I was here on furlough just after Gettysburg. Why don't you get it through your head that even if I joined the Roswell Guards here in Georgia, my regiment's stationed in Virginia. So that's where I have to go now— Virginia! I know you want me to look out for the family, but I can't stay. If they don't shoot army deserters straight off, they brand 'em with a red-hot iron on the forehead with *D* for 'deserter.' If the bluebellies come here, you'll be defended by the Confederate soldiers that are around Atlanta now. There're probably some Virginia boys in Atlanta defendin' Georgia while I'm in Virginia."

As I had told him before, I said again, "Well, it don't make good sense to me."

He had the last word. "Soldierin' and war don't make sense to women ever. Just you look at Rosellen, now. You leave her be for a spell, Hannalee." He was off onto her again.

I went into the dark house with Mama's cold water, heavy of heart. Davey wasn't like I remembered him. He didn't laugh now the way he had the first time he'd come home to us on furlough. He'd skylarked a bit with Jem and me then, but this time he sometimes looked at the two of us like we were folks he didn't even know. His temper was hotter, and he was more set in his ways. His brooding over Rosellen wouldn't make him more loving-natured on his last day at home with us, either.

As I climbed the stairs, feeling the coldness of the water through the crockery of the cup, I heard Jem breathing hard in deep sleep. He would be fresh as a frisky cat tomorrow at work, but not me. And I'd bet a penny with anybody that Rosellen would want for sleep, too. I heard that she'd told other mill-hand girls she hoped to marry Davey Reed when he came home next time from the war. He had probably riled her greatly when he had said no again to hopping the twig with her.

The ringing from the mill's bell tower woke me at four o'clock. Jem and I had to be there at five to start work. I rubbed the sleep from my eyes and looked at Mama, who was still sleeping, with her back to me. I dressed as fast as I could, trying not to wake her. Holding my shoes so as not to make noise on the steps, I went down to the kitchen. Jem was sitting at the table drinking a glass of milk from the pantry pitcher. He was the only one there, and I wondered where Davey was.

Jem told me before I could ask. "Davey was here, but he left. He said he was goin' to the churchyard to visit Pap's grave."

I nodded. I reckoned Davey was going there to say farewell to Pap before he left. Jem finished his milk as I drank mine, then I picked up my alphabet book from a chair and we left the house together.

It was a fine, bright, sun-up day outside. Later on, it would turn June-hot, but now it was a pleasure. I could hear birds singing in the trees along the creek and smell the flowers in the gardens as we went toward the mill. It was just a couple minutes' walk from our house. Other mill workers were on their way there, too.

Two spinning girls whom I knew came up abreast of Jem and me. They were dressed in brown homespun with aprons pinned to their dress fronts. The taller one asked me, "Are Rosellen and Davey goin' to hop the twig today? We thought maybe they'd get married in the mill the way most folks do 'cause it's the biggest place in town."

Her question didn't set well with me. It wasn't any of

her business. I told her, "I dunno, Sulene. Besides, we better get along if we're not goin' to be late. The Frenchman don't take to that. We're makin' Confederate gray for the soldiers here in Roswell and that's mighty important work."

The other spinner hadn't liked what I'd said. She sniffed, "My, my, don't Miss Hannalee have a lot to say this fine mornin', though? All Sulene asked was a pleasant question. You'd think the mill was all you ever thought about, and you're just a bobbin girl doin' a job just about anybody twelve years old like you can do." She ran ahead, and Sulene ran with her.

I kept my temper. What she had said was true. I was only a bobbin girl and Jem a lap boy, but someday I'd be a spinner like them and make the thread. After that I'd become a drawing girl like Rosellen, who set the patterns in the cloth. That was the best job in the whole mill. In time Jem would be a mechanic and carpenter in the mill repair shop and look after the machines the way Pap and Davey had done before the war. That was the kind of work Reed men did. Reed women worked as bobbin girls at first, then moved up to better work, as Mama had when she had been a mill hand. Once she had the baby, she would find a woman to look after him and then she'd come back to the mill. If she worked, too, we would be able to keep the house the millowners rented to Pap.

We Reeds did think a great deal about the mill. Why

not? It was important to us. It fed us and clothed us and gave us a roof over our heads. For us and a lot of folks in Roswell, the mill was the most important thing in town. It was also the biggest. Made of brick, it was four stories high and broad. Its big glass windows let in a lot of light. During the winter, the mill got lamp oil from the government and we worked by lamplight. The only times we didn't work was when Vickerys' Creek froze up so the mill wheel couldn't turn, or during a dry spell in summer when the creek water was down so low that no water came over the twenty-foot-tall mill wheel. Those were bad, worrisome times because then no money at all came in.

As I ran over the covered bridge and through the front gate into the mill yard, past the picking and dyeing buildings, the tannery, and the warehouses, I went by little, dark-bearded Mr. Roche, the Frenchman. The mill-owners had told him to run the mill for them while they were gone. He was to keep on weaving both the special gray cloth for Confederate officers' uniforms and the heavy cloth for tents, and to keep making rope, too. Pap had said the Confederacy badly needed the things our mill made. Knowing that I helped make them made me proud.

Mr. Roche didn't know my name or Jem's, and I didn't expect him to, since there were four hundred folks working in the mill. Yet he generally smiled at us young ones when he saw us, but not this morning. He was talking to a man in a brown frock coat next to him. I heard him saying in his strange-sounding foreign voice, "But, monsieur, I tell you I saw fires in the night sky, the fires of artillery! If I can see such things here at all, the enemy is too near again to please me. You say I need not worry because the Federal troops will be stopped by your magnificent army long before they come here to Roswell, but I cannot help but be concerned."

Jem had also heard him and asked me, "Were there fires in the sky last night, Hannalee? What's artillery?"

"Cannons, Jemmie. I saw the fires, too. But Davey told me not to fret over 'em."

"Then I won't fret, either," said Jem as he left me to go up the steps to the carding room. He worked there all day, carrying cans of carded lapping to the mill workers who needed them.

I went up the steps I had climbed four times a day for the last two years. By now the mill was a familiar place to me, and my work much easier than it had been at first. As I reached the sunny, fourth-story spinning room where my bobbin box was, the mill bell rang out "One, two, three, four, and five." It was time to begin work. I'd be here till seven, then go home for breakfast and return in a half hour. At twelve I'd go home for lunch and be back in forty-five minutes, then work until seven at night.

The noise began! By now I was almost used to it. The millhouse shook and boomed and throbbed with noise like the beat of a heart that was scared of something. When one of the twenty spinning girls in the room wanted me to fetch her empty bobbins to put onto either of the two thread-spinning machines she worked at, she'd signal to me with her hand. Then I'd come running down the aisle between the machines with my bobbin box. I couldn't hear anybody speaking, or even yelling, on this floor, so I had to look for hand signals.

It wasn't too bad. I didn't generally work more than fifteen minutes out of every hour. The rest of the time I sat on the stool beside my box and looked at my ABC book. Before the new preacher had come and his wife had started teaching, I'd taken my knitting to the mill and made stockings and mittens for Pap and Davey. Mama wanted me to learn writing and reading and, most of all, arithmetic. Then maybe someday, when I was older, I could work in the office and keep the mill's records. She'd be proud of me if the owners had me working in the office, especially since girls generally didn't work there. Mama had high hopes for me and wanted me to make much more than the two dollars a week I was making now as a bobbin girl.

I put the Yankees and Davey and Rosellen out of my mind and studied the alphabet, every now and then looking up to see if anybody had need of a bobbin. I worked till the breakfast bell rang, then hurried home to eat the corn bread, bacon, and chicory-and-ground-up-peas coffee Mama had fixed for us. Davey was upstairs sleeping, and Mama said she doubted if he would be down for noontime, either. I kept quiet about Rosellen, reckoning he would tell her himself when he had a mind to. I ate fast so I'd get back to the mill on time.

At noon Jem and I ran home again and ate more corn bread. We sniffed the good smell of the old hen that Mama had killed to stew for our supper. Davey still wasn't there when we left again for the mill.

By the end of the day I was weary of running and sitting and running again. Sometimes, even when nobody signaled to me, I'd lift my head to watch the spinners reach over their machines to straighten the roving, and I would hold my breath. This was why all of the mill girls pulled their hair back and held it fast. Long hair could pull a person into a machine and hurt her bad. Pap had said every mill floor was dangerous in some way. The brass-tipped, fast-moving wooden shuttles could misfire and hit a girl weaver. Fingers that didn't move fast enough could get broken. Many a man had lost his arm being careless with the working gears of the great mill wheel.

At seven of evening the mill bell rang for the last time, and the machinery was turned off for the day. I ran downstairs and waited in the mill yard for Jem, so we could walk home together as always. He'd got there ahead of me. I saw him a distance away talking with Rosellen.

As I came toward them, Rosellen turned to look at me. Her face was whiter than usual. Drawing out her words as tight as the threads she worked with all day, she said, "I'll tell you, Hannalee, what I just now told your brother. I'm not comin' to your house tonight to any chicken dinner, even if I haven't tasted chicken for two years now. I'm not goin' to tell Davey farewell with a kiss on his mouth. I won't be home to him if he comes to my house, either. If he won't have me, I won't have any part of him."

Suddenly her face crumpled like an old piece of cloth. Tears came to her eyes. She turned about and half ran away from Jem and me. She jerked the pins from her honey-yellow hair and let it fall down her back. It floated behind her as she ran through the gate, headed for the house where she lived with her Aunt Marilla.

As Jem and I walked home, he asked me what the trouble between Davey and Rosellen was. I told him what I'd overheard the night before and of my talk with Davey outside the house.

Jem said to me, "I wish Davey wasn't goin' back to the war."

"So do I. Virginia's a long ways away, Jemmie."

When we came in the front door, Corporal Howell Quint was there, sitting in Pap's rocking chair. He and Davey were drinking corn whiskey, while Mama stood at our iron cookstove in her long white apron, lifting the lid off the stewpot full of chicken and dumplings.

Howell, a freckly man, was dressed in his gray uniform. I liked him even though I'd met him only once before, when Davey had fetched him home on Howell's way to Marietta on furlough. He was a mighty friendly sort. He hailed me with, "Here's purty little Hannalee come home." He leaned over the table to ask Davey, "When'll I be meetin' the light of your life, this Rosellen you're always jawin' about in camp?"

This made me say, "Davey, I need to talk to you in private."

He gave me a strange look but got up off his stool and led me out back to where we'd been last night.

"Is it about Rosellen? Did you see her at the mill?"

"Yes, we did—Jem and me. She says to tell you she won't come here tonight and she don't want you to go to her house."

"Is that all she had to say?"

"She said she wasn't goin' to tell you farewell with a kiss on your mouth, and if you don't want her, she don't want you."

Davey let out a long, sorrowful, and at the same time angry breath. I touched him on the arm and said, "She was carryin' on when she ran away from Jem and me. She cares for you." I wanted to talk about something else, so I asked, "What'd Howell have to say about the red fires in the sky? Did he see 'em, too, from where he lives?"

"No, he said he got too full of squirrel-head whiskey last night at home to see anythin'. His kinfolks told him about 'em in the morning, though. A Confederate cavalryman passin' through their town told them that there's a battle goin' on at Kennesaw Mountain. There's nothin' to worry about here, though. We held the Yankees back at the mountain. Besides, there's a lot of our army between here and there. Now, tell me how Rosellen was carryin' on. Was she in a big stew like last night?"

"No, she was weepin', Davey."

As he leaned against the side of the door, he shrugged his shoulders, coughed, and said, "I guess that proves somethin' if she cries tears over me. I'll let her be for the time I'm here. I won't go lookin' for her."

After Davey and I came back inside, I told Mama not to expect Rosellen for dinner. Davey asked Howell to come out the front way and they were gone for a time. I knew Davey was telling his friend about Rosellen. When they came back inside, they sat down together to supper with never a word said from anybody about her again. I liked Howell. He could have teased Davey, but he didn't.

While we all ate the old hen, we listened to the men talk about the war and generals Longstreet and Lee. Suddenly Howell asked Jem, "Did your big brother ever tell you about the time old Longstreet got himself wounded and old Gen'ral Robert E. Lee decided to lead a charge of cavalry himself? Texas soldiers grabbed hold of Lee's bridle and stopped his horse from goin' on ahead."

Jem's mouth was wide open as he said, "No, he didn't."

"Well, now you heard it. That happened a couple of times. Nobody's as brave as old Robert E. Lee."

Howell did most of the talking. He had a way about him that was funny where Davey didn't anymore. When supper was over, the two of them started in on the whiskey again, and I noticed that Davey took a lot more of it than usual.

When Davey had just poured himself a full cup, Howell said, laughing, "Say, Davey, do you recall the times at Sharpsburg you told me that you wished you was a dwarf?"

"Uh-huh, I recall that, Howell."

I asked, "Davey, why would you want that?"

Howell explained, laughing again. "Because there'd be a lot less of a person's body to get shot at."

"That's right, Howell, we been lucky."

Howell went on. "More'n once I counted all my sinnin's in one minute durin' the time I was fightin' Yankees. I wonder if the Yankee boys do that, too?"

Jem put in fast, "Oh no, Yankee boys are outright, all-day Sunday cowards. They don't stop to fight. They run off and hide."

Davey told him, "No, Jem. They can scrap pretty good when they have it in mind to. Do you want me to hand the bottle to you, Howell?"

Jem and Mama and I went up to bed an hour or so later,

but we could hear Davey and Howell below finishing off the whiskey. Their voices kept getting louder and louder, and finally they began to sing. Davey had a good singing voice, something he'd got from Pap. He sang one song I liked a real lot, and I reckoned I knew why he was singing it:

> *"Aura Lee! Aura Lee!*
> *Maid of golden hair,*
> *Sunshine came along with thee,*
> *And swallows in the air. . . ."*

He made the song as sad as he was feeling about Rosellen.

When we all came down the next morning at the clanging of the mill bell, there was nothing in the room to let us know that the two of them had ever been there except for the two cups and empty jug on the table. Davey's army coat and his gray peaked soldier cap were gone from the pegs where he'd hung them.

Jem cried out, "Davey went away without sayin' anythin' to anybody."

Before I could say a word, Mama told us, "That must have been the easiest way for him to go." She put her hand over her belly and sighed. Then she went on, "Your pa gave us a lovin' farewell last time he was home. That was his way. No matter, this is Davey's way. It don't mean he hasn't any feelin's for us. I'll fetch some milk now so you'll have somethin' in your stomachs before you go to the mill. Jem, and you, too, Hannalee, I think you best keep away from Rosellen Sanders for a while."

As she went to the pantry for the milk pitcher, she suddenly turned around and said, "I think I'll go talk to her Aunt Marilla sometime later on and see how the wind blows. This trouble between Rosellen and Davey don't run on all fours with me; and there's more devilment on my mind, too. Last night I stuck my head out the window to see if I could see those red fires Davey had told me about yesterday, and I spied 'em. I don't like this fightin' goin' on at Kennesaw Mountain. It's too close to here to comfort me." She ordered us fiercely, "You both pray for Davey that he comes back to us again."

I nodded my head but didn't say anything. All through the war I'd prayed for him and for Pap, too, but Pap had never come home to us alive again.

Chapter Two

Gray Coat—Blue Coat

DAVEY AND HOWELL LEFT ON A WEDNESDAY, AND JEM and me and everybody else went to the mill to work. That day Jem and I minded what Mama and Davey had said about leaving Rosellen be, and we did our work as usual. We went back and forth to our floors in the mill Thursday and Friday, too, and never once saw hide nor hair of Rosellen.

We heard about her, though, when we came home after work Saturday to find her aunt sitting with Mama, rocking back and forth. White-headed Marilla Sanders, whose age nobody really knew, greeted Jem and me friendly as ever and said, "I come to visit your ma and fetch her news. There could maybe be Confederate soldiers comin' here tomorrow to keep an eye on the town. This mornin' the Frenchman at the mill told Rosellen that he'd heard it from somebody who knows, and she fetched the news home to me when she came home to eat at noon."

Jem asked, "Where'd they be comin' from—Virginia?"

Mama told him sharply, "No, Jem, they'll be comin' here from around Atlanta, it's the closest place. It won't be Davey comin' here again so soon."

"Oh." Jem wasn't happy at what he heard, and neither was I.

Marilla went on, "Even if Davey Reed was to come here with the soldiers, I doubt my Rosellen would throw herself at him right then. She says she don't want any part of you Reeds. Her dander's up. I reckon she'll get over it 'fore long, though. I know the girl. She's proud. She's got a temper hot as fire." Marilla got up slowly. "You know I don't share her views about you. If I did, I wouldn't have come here today. I hope there's no hard feelin's between you and me. We always been friendly to each other."

Mama said, "No, Marilla, we don't hold bad feelin's. We hope Davey and Rosellen'll tie the knot someday. It's somethin' that's been expected of 'em since they were Jem's age." She shook her head. "I don't like our soldiers comin' here, though. Why send 'em here from Atlanta unless trouble's expected?"

Marilla nodded, then said, "That's what Rosellen said the Frenchman told her and the other drawin' girls. He said the millowners telegraphed him from Savannah and told him to keep on runnin' the mill like always. He also told her that the Yankees left off fightin' at Kennesaw Mountain and circled around it. They're comin' on to Smyrna, maybe to fight on different ground."

I said, "Smyrna's nearer to Roswell than Kennesaw Mountain. Do they think the Yankees will come here, too?"

Hearing this, Jem got all excited. He jumped up and down, shouting, "I bet there's goin' to be a battle here! We'll be in a battle, just like Davey was!"

This riled Mama plenty. She came over to Jem, got hold of him, and shook him hard as she cried, "You don't know what you're talkin' about! Don't you go hopin' for battles hereabouts. You just pray hard that there won't be any in your whole life. Losin' your pa and worryin' over your brother's enough for anybody. If soldiers come here to Roswell, you don't go near them, you hear? They don't need pesterin' from you."

Marilla Sanders chuckled. "Boys'll be boys, Delia!" She asked Jem, "If the Yankees do come, what'll you fight 'em with, a slingshot, the way old King David did in the Bible?"

"A pitchfork. I'll borrow one. That's the right thing to use on bluebelly Yankee devils." The minute after he'd said this, Jem ran out the back door so Mama couldn't swat him with her hand.

We all went to church on Sunday and heard a sermon on being brave in the time of trouble and staying true to the Confederacy. Later that afternoon, still dressed in my Sunday-best blue calico, I started off to the preacher's house with Jem and three mill-hand girls for our reading, arithmetic, and writing lessons. While we were walking there, we heard a clopping of hooves that meant lots of horses were coming down the road. Jem, who had been mumbling his ABC's, hushed up, and we all stood together waiting for them. Confederate cavalry came riding toward us. The officers wore gray uniforms, made from the cloth we wove for them here in Roswell; but the other men mostly wore clothes of butternut brown, a color that was dyed at home. Mr. Roche had been right —soldiers had come to town.

Jem sucked in his breath and gave them a cheer.

The soldiers noticed us then, after that yell, but not one of them smiled or waved. They only looked at us as they went past, their harness gear clinking.

A mill girl older than me told us, "I heard there might be some fightin' around here. There ain't many men fightin' age in Roswell anymore, so the gen'ral in Atlanta has sent us some of his soldiers." She stopped for a spell, then went on. "I was in Atlanta last month. The soldiers there smiled at folks when they cheered them. These don't appear to be happy about comin' here. I wonder why."

The soldiers made a camp down by Vickerys' Creek, where it joins the Chattahoochee River, so we didn't see much of them in town. Our little Home Guard of old men and young boys my age went to visit them, but the cavalry didn't seem to want their help, so back they came.

One thing the soldiers did do was to cut the grain for us in the fields around town, and we all were grateful to them.

Sunday night there was a red blazing in the sky again. I saw it when I went out to the privy and reckoned that, from the direction, it came from Smyrna way. Rosellen's aunt had been right. There was fighting going on.

Jem and I went to work on Monday even if it was July the Fourth. Making Confederate gray was more important than having picnics and celebrations. Besides, there wasn't anything to eat that was worth making a fuss over cooking. We ate mostly corn bread and sowbelly now.

When the two of us started for the mill Tuesday morning, we had to dodge around the cavalry horses moving up and down the road. Soldiers kept yelling at us to give way, and we did. For the first time in a long while I spied Rosellen. She was standing near the mill gate looking at the soldiers, and she had a frown on her face. The minute she saw me, she hurried through the gate.

When Jem and I came out at seven to go home for breakfast, Jem suddenly grabbed me by one arm and halted me. He pointed and cried, "Look over there, Hannalee! Look at the smoke. There's somethin' on fire down by the river."

Something surely was. A big tower of gray smoke was rising in the air, but none of the folks I saw on the street were running to the fire.

I yelled at a group of old men who were just standing in a bunch looking at the smoke, "Maybe somebody's been burned up alive down there."

"No, it's not a house, child!" one told me. "It's the covered bridge over the Chattahoochee. The soldiers are burnin' it."

"The Yankees have come here?" I cried.

He shook his head, looking sad. "No, our boys are doin' it. They've set fires under it at both ends. They're destroyin' it so the Yankees can't use it to cross over to us. Go home now, both of you."

While Jem and I were standing there, still looking at the smoke, Mr. Roche came hurrying up to us. He said, "Go home, children. Go home and stay there. Don't come back to the mill."

Jem cried, "Mr. Roche, are the Yankees comin' here?"

"We think so. The telegraph says they're near. Our soldiers are leaving here as soon as they've finished with the bridge."

Yankees? Bluebelly Yankees coming here? Scared to death, I grabbed hold of Jem's hand, and we ran home.

Mama was waiting at the front of the house. She gathered us in to her and wrapped her arms around us. "Oh, my God, oh, my God, what'll happen to us? Our soldiers are leavin' us to the Yankees."

I cried, "Mama, Mama, Mr. Roche told us not to go back to the mill. Where'll we go?"

I looked up into her face. Right then it was just the

way it had been when the wagon bringing home the box with Pap inside it had arrived. Not only were there tears in her eyes, but her face was pulled all out of shape, so she didn't look like herself at all.

All at once she went poker-stiff, and I felt her hands clutching at me. She told us, "We owe it to your pa to keep our heads no matter what happens." Her face was her own face again, and there was spite in her voice as she went on, "Look behind you! Look at the wagons and buggies leavin' town, children. Look at the folks runnin' around now like chickens with their heads just cut off when they'd do best to go home and stay there."

I turned around to see. What she had said was true. Jem and I had been some of the first ones out of the mill. Now others had come out and heard the news. They'd seen the smoke and learned what it meant. People who had got the news earlier and who had horses and mules were leaving town, their wagons clattering along. Other folks, mostly girl mill hands, were racing up and down like crazy people, waving their hands in the air. They would run up to Mr. Roche, talk to him, then run around some more. Finally they would head for their homes, and other scared mill girls would come up to him.

Mama said to us, "Look at me, you two. We're goin' to stay right here in this house when the Yankees come. We won't give 'em a speck of trouble. We won't run away. Where could we go where they won't find us if they want us? We'll act brave." Her hands were trembling now as she let go of us. "Besides, what will Yankees do here? There ain't nobody here to put up a fight. I bet they'll ride right on through on their way to someplace important. What would they want with womenfolks and boys and old men? We won't give 'em trouble, and they won't give us trouble. Let's go inside. You can watch from the upstairs windows. If our Home Guard gives 'em a fight and there's any shootin', you can come down straight away and we'll go into the root cellar. Davey told me that's where folks stay when battles are goin' on."

The three of us went inside, shut the front and back doors, and put chairs in front of them. While Mama sat below, Jem and I went upstairs to our own rooms and took a place each at a window. We ate the pieces of corn bread she had put out as our breakfast.

The yelling outside died down, and after a time there wasn't anybody on the road at all. It seemed like the whole town was holding its breath, waiting, the way I was. I waited and waited with the hairs on the back of my head and neck prickling. I thought about what Davey and Pap had said about the bluebellies. I'd never seen a Yankee, but I reckoned they'd be different from us Georgia folks, even if they spoke English like us. I didn't expect them to be friendly to us either, since there was a war going on between us and them. How I hoped Mama was right about the bluebellies riding straight through Roswell.

*   *   *

They came in the middle of the day—bluecoat cavalry mounted on big black horses. Some had bright swords glittering in their hands like they were ready to cut anybody down who tried to stand up to them. The horses were wet up to the withers from fording the river now that the bridge was gone. The soldiers looked up at windows as they rode. They must have been expecting somebody to shoot at them, because some of them had very big, long-barreled pistols in their hands. I held my breath. I wanted to duck down behind my windowsill but didn't. If I moved, one of them might shoot at my head.

I hissed loudly to Jem, who was only a couple feet away at the window in his room, "Jemmie, you stay put where you are. Don't move till they're gone."

"I'll stay put, Hannalee. I won't move!" He sure sounded scared.

I didn't try to count the number of soldiers after I got up to a hundred. There were too many of them to go on counting.

When the last of the riders had gone, I told Jem, "We better get down to Mama now." I had to pry my fingers from the windowsill before I could move, and when Jem came out of his room, his face had gone white as a summer cloud.

He whispered, "There's sure plenty of bluebellies come here. There's lots more of 'em than there was of the Confederates."

That was a truth if I had ever heard one. I nodded, and down we went to sit beside Mama at the table and wait. We kept our ears tuned for noises, but mostly we waited for the sound of the Yankees leaving once they had looked over the town. The sound of their horses moving out would be the welcomest sound I'd ever heard yet, but it didn't come. I didn't hear anything but the *creak-creak*-ing of Mama's rocking chair and the clicking of her knitting needles as she knit more socks for Davey. The mill was dead quiet, so quiet I could make myself believe it was Sunday, not Tuesday at all.

Mama didn't fix any lunch or supper, since we weren't hungry at all. We still sat together at the table. We didn't talk or even look at one another. Finally Mama said softly, "The baby's waitin' on the Yankees, too. He hasn't kicked in a long time now."

Just after she said that, there came a hard banging sound on the front door, like somebody was knocking on it with the butt end of a horse pistol. *Yankees!* It had to be. Nobody we knew ever hit a door that way.

Mama got up. She told us, "Remember now. Watch what you say and do."

The minute she opened the door, two Yankee soldiers came in fast, with drawn pistols pointed at us. The shorter, red-faced one asked, "Are there any men in this house? Any Rebel, Secesh, soldiers?"

Mama did us proud as she answered him. "No, sir. My

husband's dead, and my oldest son's in the Army of the Confederacy in Virginia. We're the Reeds, and we three are all there are in this house."

The short soldier said, "Private Andrews, see if this woman's lying. Search the house. Look under the beds to see if there are any cowardly Seceshes hidden there."

We watched as the tall bluebelly went poking through the downstairs and then ran up to clump around over our heads.

When he came back down again and went to search the backyard, the short soldier asked, "Are there any mill workers in this house? Are you a mill hand, woman?"

"No, sir, not right now." Mama pointed to Jem and me and said, "My children work in the mill."

"How old are you, girlie?" the soldier asked me.

"Twelve, and my brother's ten. I'm a bobbin girl and he's a lap boy."

He grunted at me, "All right, that's enough for General Garrard to know. Woman, you can stay here in the house, but you brats are to come along with me."

"What do you want with my children?" Mama cried.

By now the other bluebelly was back, standing in our back door, grinning. He'd pulled off one of Pap's red roses and stuck it in his cap. He answered Mama. "We got orders to round up every one of the mill hands, big and little, and take them to the town square now. General Garrard wants 'em." He waved his pistol at us. "So you sprouts had better get a move on."

"Ma!" shouted Jem and ran for her, but the tall Yankee got him by the collar before he could reach her. Kicking his feet, Jem was dragged out the back door.

Mama screamed, "What do you want with them? They're children!"

The short bluebelly told her coldly, "General Garrard's come here to see that the mills quit running. One way to do that is to see to it that there aren't any people to work in them."

Mama fell down into the front-door chair the Yankees had kicked out of their way when they'd come inside. She acted like the short bluebelly had kicked her. She whispered softly, "You wouldn't shoot children—not even Yankees would do that. They're not much more than babies." She put her hand on her belly and moaned.

In the same hard, cold voice he'd used before, the Yankee told her, "That's up to Uncle Billy Sherman. He's head of the Union Army in these parts. He might have 'em shot." The soldier stepped up to me and ordered, "Come along, girlie. You're wanted at the town square, too. Say good-bye to your mama."

I went to Mama and got down onto my knees beside her. Too scared to cry, I hugged her and she hugged me. Then she did something mighty strange. She jerked one of the persimmon-seed buttons off the top of her dress and gave it to me. She told me softly, "They won't shoot you and Jem. I just know they won't. But I think they'll take you away from here, God knows where. Wherever you go, keep this to remind yourself to come home. Turn your heart to me. Turn homeward, Hannalee! Promise me."

"I promise you, Mama." I took the button into my hand and made a fist over it.

The Yankee snapped at me, "That's long enough. Let's go, girlie."

I let go of Mama and she of me. I ran past the soldier, stumbling out into the red-hot July sunshine, with him coming along at my heels. I held tight as could be to the persimmon-seed button.

When I got to the town square, I saw that it was full of people. Some were old men mill hands, but mostly there were girls, looking as scared as I was, flocked together like chickens afraid of a fox. Yankee soldiers, some on horseback, some on foot, surrounded them. Now and then the bluebelly lines would open up to let a new prisoner through. My soldier grabbed hold of my arm and shoved me between two big Yankees into a bunch of weeping mill-hand girls.

"Hannalee! Hannalee!" came a cry I knew right off. It was Jem's voice.

I called out to him, "Jemmie, I'm here! I'll find you!" and I began to duck around among the women, looking for him. Before I found him, though, somebody grabbed hold of me by the shoulders. I froze where I stood, looking down at the hand that held me. Then I looked up into Rosellen Sanders's pure-white face. Her eyes were glittery green as she whispered to me, "You stay with me, Hannalee. We'll find Jem, and we'll all stay together, no matter what happens. You listen to what I tell you, and you do what I say to do."

I told her, "They left Mama home. Did they take your Aunt Marilla?"

"No, all they want is mill hands. It's the mill that brought 'em here. They're gonna burn it."

"Burn the mill?" If they did that, what would feed us Reeds?

Sick to my stomach, I looked over my other shoulder. A Yankee soldier stood nearby. He was a tall, dark-mustached one with a shiny-visor blue cap and bright brass buttons on his blue coat. He wasn't looking at me but at Rosellen. He filled his eyes up with her, then called out to the soldier next to him, "I never in my whole life saw so many good-looking women all together in one place before."

Rosellen heard him. He'd meant for her to. Her finger-nails bit deeper into my shoulder, hurting me. She said, "Let's get away from this spot and find Jem. We'll go to the middle of the square. You call out for your brother."

I did, and he came pushing through to us pretty soon. At first he didn't know what to make of Rosellen's being with me. Then, when she opened her arms to him, he ran to her and hugged her about the mid-section. She told him softly, "Don't you bawl, Jemmie. We're gonna sit ourselves down on the ground right here and wait. I been thinkin'. It's hot as billy bedamned, and the Yankees feel it the same way we do. They're standin' up, but we'll sit down to save our strength and let 'em waste theirs. Sit down, you two."

There was a fierceness in her voice that made us obey her. We sat down in the hot dust of the square. A minute later, Rosellen began to pick up dirt and rub it onto her face, neck, and arms.

She told me in a hiss, "Hannalee, you and Jem pick up dirt, too, and throw it in my hair. Make me look brown-headed and dirty. I don't want that big, dark bluebelly to know me by sight again." Her voice got even lower as she went on, "I never wanted to take up with Davey Reed's kin ever again, and look at me now. I'm nothin' to him."

I put Mama's persimmon-seed button into my deep apron pocket where it would be safe. I told her, "You're his own true love, Rosellen Sanders. He told me that just before he left."

Jem added, "Davey'll come save us from the bluebellies."

Rosellen was fiercer than ever now. She flared at us. "No he won't. Our soldiers won't come here to save us. They can't. I don't think there are enough of 'em here in Georgia to do that. I heard tell there are some three thousand Yankees here right now, mebbe more. As for bein' his true love, hush yourself about that, Hannalee. I don't want to hear that kind of talk. I'm lookin' after you and Jem because you Reeds and us Sanderses have been friends a long time, that's why. Now you get that red dirt onto me fast as ever you can, and you promise me that you'll do what I tell you to do. You bear in mind that I ain't Davey's wife and I ain't your ma, so you better not sass me like you could your kinfolks."

"No, ma'am," said Jem, lifting both of his dirt-filled hands, letting the dirt sift down onto Rosellen's golden hair. It turned brownish red in no time at all. Now her hair was dull, and there was nothing pretty and shiny about it to make anybody take notice of her.

Some other girls had been watching us and now they hunkered down, too, and started to rub dirt onto their arms and necks. Most of them were weeping, though, so it wouldn't do them much good to dirty their faces, because their tears would make streaks in the dust. Rosellen wasn't crying. She had the kind of eyes that changed with the way she felt. Now they weren't angry green or quiet gray. They had gone so dark you couldn't say what color they were. They seemed to be looking somewheres nobody could see but herself. Her eyes were so strange they made me shiver. This wasn't a Rosellen I'd ever known before.

"Wait," she told us, "sit here and wait. The Yankees

have cut our telegraph wires to Savannah and Atlanta. I seen 'em do it. They're fixin' up their own so they can send messages to their head gen'ral—somebody named Sherman—the Yankees call him 'Cump.' " Rosellen drew in a deep breath. "I think the gen'ral who's here in Roswell is askin' Sherman what he wants to do with us now. A while ago I heard one Yankee tell another one that they plan to keep us here in the town square till they get some word about us."

I asked, "Will we be here at night, too?"

"I reckon so. They went to a lot of trouble to gather us all together. They took me out of the mill. I'd taken my lunch to eat there. Mr. Roche tried to make 'em think the mill was French and belonged to a neutral country by putting up the French flag, but they weren't fooled. He didn't fly the Northern flag beside his own, and that gave him away. They are surely riled up about him. Maybe they'll hang him. But we'd better be quiet now. Stay down, or the heat'll make you faint dead away. There are pumps here beside the horse waterin' troughs, so we won't die of thirst or have to beg the bluebellies for a drink of water."

Jem asked, "Rosellen, will they feed us? Where'll we sleep? What if I have to go to the privy?"

For the first time Rosellen laughed. She said, "If they plan to keep us alive, they'll have to feed us and let us do some things. As for sleepin', unless they take us into some of the buildin's, we'll sleep right here on the ground. It ain't as if we'll freeze at night."

I said, "Maybe they'll let folks who ain't mill workers fetch us blankets and pillows and shawls."

"No!" Rosellen shook her head, making the dust fly out of her hair. "An old woman tried to fetch her daughter's little baby here so it could be nursed, but the Yankees pushed her back. They won't let nobody through to us, not even a nursin' baby."

Jem wailed softly, "Why? What do they want us for?"

"Because we made cloth and rope. That's what the Yankee who grabbed hold of me and the other hands in the mill told us. He said we was all guilty of treason against the United States of America because we helped the Confederacy by makin' cloth. He said we was foul traitors, and the penalty for traitors was death."

I cried out softly but, remembering what Mama said, I told her, "Mama doesn't think they'll shoot us. She says they plan to take us away. Mama knows how things will turn out sometimes. She says it's her Indian blood tellin' her."

Rosellen nodded, grim as could be. "That's most likely what they will do. Shootin' some four hundred unarmed women, old men, and young 'uns won't make this Gen'ral Sherman's army look proud. No, not even Yankee horse soldiers would do that. Be quiet now. Rest."

Jem and I obeyed her. We sat in the dirt next to her

and didn't move. As the day went on, the other mill hands dropped down, too. Eventually hundreds of us were sitting, covering our heads with our hands against the hot sun. Only a few of us had sunbonnets, and some folks fainted from the heat.

We were completely circled by bluebellies, standing close together so nobody could get past them. They were armed and ready to shoot at us, and they didn't take their eyes off us for a minute. I never saw so much dark blue cloth before in my whole life.

There wasn't any supper for us.

The Yankees built bonfires around the square and watched us all night long. When we needed to relieve ourselves we had to ask a Yankee to go with us to a privy. While we were inside, he stayed just outside the door. Rosellen went with me twice, then I went with Jem once and she went the second time. Each time I went, all the Yankee guard ever said was "Hurry up, you Seceshes!" I knew what "Secesh" meant. It meant that our state had seceded from the Union and was a bad name to the Yankees.

We mill hands lay flat on the dirt, which still held the heat of the day, and we tried to sleep. Rosellen didn't tell me to say my prayers, but she didn't have to. I said them all by myself, speaking so softly nobody could hear me. I blessed Davey as I always did, but this time I also asked for blessings for Mama and the baby to come, and for Jem,

Rosellen, and myself, too, though that was selfish of me to want them for myself.

Rosellen only wept once in the night, and she didn't make much noise at it, either. When I rolled over to her because I was crying, I heard her sounds. She folded me into her arms. When I rose up onto one elbow later on, I saw that Jem was curled up to her back.

The sound of galloping horses woke me up at the break of the day. Other mill girls were sitting up as well, and so was Rosellen. She tugged at Jem's shoulder to rouse him, too.

The Yankees around us were standing guard just as they had been all night, but beyond them a swarm of bluecoat soldiers were moving around, their heads turned to the road where the horses were coming.

My heart jumped up in me. Were they our soldiers coming to fight these Yankees? No, it was more bluecoats, some twenty of them, with two wagons. I watched a young-looking officer with gold boards on his shoulders and a black slouch hat come out of our general store and go over to the newcomers. One of them gave him a black leather bag. The officer took the bag inside the store, then some bluebellies went over to look inside the wagons.

One of them yelled out, "Whiskey, boys. By gum, they fetched us whiskey. Now, wasn't that nice of the generals?"

I heard Rosellen suck in her breath, then, shaking her head, she said, "Whiskey, oh, my God! Lord help us if they start in on that!"

The Yankees fed us hard, dry corn bread for breakfast, passing it out to us as we filed along a table they had piled high with it. That was all they gave us. As we took ours, Rosellen ordered, "Eat it. Eat every crumb even if it busts your teeth."

That morning things began to happen. The Yankees started burning what they took out of the mill. They piled up tables and chairs, cloth, ropes, and bobbins, and set fire to the lot. They burned the red, blue, and white bar flag Mr. Roche had run up over the mill. I heard that they had put him into the town jail. We watched the Yankees set fire to the buildings around the square and, using coal oil, fire the wooden floors of the mill itself.

Not only was it hot as the day went on, it got hard to breathe because of all the smoke. The bonfires added to the heat, and sweat poured off of us even though we didn't move around.

Near noon a red-bearded Yankee officer came up to us. He climbed onto a table and read to us in a loud voice from a sheet of paper: "By order of General Sherman, commanding officer of the United States Army in the seceded state of Georgia, you are all under arrest for making cloth and rope for the Confederate States of America. You are all traitors to the Union. To make sure that you will not be able to continue your traitorous work, you are all to be taken away from here to Indiana and set at liberty there. This means each and every one of you mill workers—men, women, and children."

Oh, what a groan came up from our throats. I clapped my hands over my eyes, threw my head back, and howled loud as ever I could in spite of Rosellen's tugging at me.

A shot fired over our heads made us hush up, and then the Yankee bellowed, "You'll be taken by wagon to Marietta, and from there to the Ohio River. Now, for your own safety sit down and don't give us any trouble."

Nobody talked anymore. We huddled together like it was freezing cold, with each one of us thinking about leaving. How far away from Roswell was Indiana? I didn't exactly know, but I figured it was a far way. Once the preacher's wife showed me a map. There were two states between Georgia and the Ohio River, Tennessee and Kentucky. On top of Kentucky was Indiana. We'd surely have to travel for days to get to Indiana through two states. Tears came to my eyes, and I looked away from Jem and Rosellen. When would the Yankees come for us with their wagons?

The wagons didn't come, not that day or for three days more. I tried to hate our soldiers for leaving us, but, truly, I couldn't find it in my heart to do it. There'd been so few of them compared to all these Yankees. If our men had made a stand and fought, they'd all most likely be dead or wounded or prisoners like us by now.

All that time we sat in the red-hot sun of the town square. The Yankees always had corn bread for us to eat, and once they parceled out some baked ham. There was never a sign, though, of the wagons that were to take us away.

Nobody from Roswell was allowed to talk to us. I worried over Mama, wondering how she was faring all by herself. I looked for her around the edges of the Yankee guards, but never once did I catch sight of her.

Between the mill fires and bonfires always smoking and blazing and my being hungry and sad, those days were a misery. On the tenth of July, in the afternoon, the blue-bellies guarding us got into the whiskey that Rosellen had never for a minute stopped worrying over. We watched the Yankees play dice for cups of whiskey and then pour it down their gullets as fast as they could when they won.

Before long the drinking soldiers began running into the crowds of mill girls and grabbing hold of some of them, whirling them around and dancing or trying to catch and kiss them. One headed straight for Rosellen. He almost got her around the waist, yelling something about "waltzing a pretty Secesh," when Jem came running up behind him and butted him in the rear with his head down. Then he ran for his life with the Yankee, sore as a boil, after him. But it was too crowded in the square, and the bluebelly was too drunk to have gotten a real good look at him.

Rosellen put a hand over my mouth as she dragged me away to the other side of the square. She said, "Don't call out Jem's name. Don't let 'em know what it is so they can find him later and punish him for what he done for me just now. Jem'll be all right if you don't."

"Oh, Rosellen!" I threw my arms around her, crying, while other Yankees with cups of whiskey in their hands came walking through us prisoners, staring into the girls' faces. I hung tight to Rosellen. They would have to pry me loose if they tried to take her away from me.

Pretty soon there was cussing and laughing and girls struggling to get away from Yankees all over the square. Sometimes one of them would scream, and then I'd see her running away from an angry bluebelly soldier that she'd slapped in the face or bitten when he tried to kiss her.

"Oh, God, where are those wagons?" I heard Rosellen cry out.

The wagons never did come. New Yankees showed up, though, fresh from burning other Georgia towns and mills. By now I had begun to think that there wasn't anything left in the world anymore but Yankee soldiers and us mill hands. Would these new soldiers join in with the drunk ones? I started to pray hard as ever I could.

My prayer got heard. These new bluebellies were dead, cold sober. It didn't take long for their officer to see what was going on in the town square. I heard him yell for his men to "halt" as they passed through town. Then he said something that I couldn't hear over all the noise.

His soldiers understood what he wanted them to do, though, and they didn't waste a minute at it, either. They rode into the crowd of us mill hands, right past the drunken bluebellies. Then they dismounted, knocking the drunkards aside with the flats of their swords if they had to. A tall, yellow-bearded, yellow-headed Yankee dismounted near Rosellen and me. He grabbed hold of me, pulling me away from her, and lifted me up onto his horse. A big soldier near him grabbed Rosellen and slung her onto his horse, too. Looking around the square, I saw that the new Yankees were doing the same thing all over the place. Girls, boys, and the old men mill hands were all being put up onto Yankee horses. Rosellen was sitting on one so close to me I could reach out and touch its mane. Her face looked surprised as well as scared. I reckoned I looked the same way, too.

As my Yankee mounted his horse, he told me, "Put your arms around my middle, little sister. I'll get you out of here before you get in a peck of trouble. Hold on tight to me."

It was on the tip of my tongue to tell him that it was the Yankees who made all the trouble, but I didn't. We trotted away with every mill hand to a rider. We passed what was left of my house. There wasn't anything now but a heap of ashes, still smoking.

Where was Mama? I yelled out for her and tried to slide down off the horse, but the Yankee reached back and caught hold of one of my knees, keeping me on.

Mama'd been sitting among some fruit trees Pap had planted, and came over to us. She was holding a bundle of clothes. She called out to me, "Where are they takin' you, Hannalee?"

"Indiana," I cried back. "They say we're goin' to Indiana. I'll be back. I've got the button. Watch out for yourself and the baby."

"I will. You watch out for Jem. I seen him and Rosellen ride by just now. They didn't hear me when I called to 'em. Don't fret over me. I'm goin' to live with Marilla Sanders now. I only waited here to see you come by."

"I'll be back, Mama!"

"Remember, Hannalee! Remember!"

As my soldier put his horse into a canter, I turned around to look back at Mama. She wasn't waving. She had her hand over the top of her dress where she'd pulled off the button I had in my apron pocket. She was weeping, and so was I.

My Yankee said, "I hail from Illinois myself. It's a good distance from here to Indiana, little sister Reb. Put that notion of getting back here while a war's on out of your head."

I didn't answer him. Curse the whole race of Yankees!

I knew that I'd try hard as I could to get back home. Not only wouldn't I forget Mama and Pap and Davey, I'd remember Roswell forever. I'd remember Vickerys' Creek falls and the mill and the slow Chattahoochee River, the bluffs, and the smell of Pap's red roses by the door. I'd never forget—never.

I made a wish on a crow flying overhead. If he didn't flap his wings till he was out of sight, I'd get my wish —to come home! That old devil of a crow flew off without one single flap and came down in Pap's peach tree.

Chapter Three

Hilly, Bumpy, and Stumpy!

I HATED MY YANKEE, AND I HATED BEING HIS PRISONER. I let go of him. At first I vowed not to say a word to him, but after a while, being careful not to touch him, I asked, "How many miles is it from here to Indiana?"

He was quiet for a little bit, then he told me, "More than four hundred as the crow flies, little sister."

As the crow flies. That crow again! This put some heart into me and gave me something to go on.

The Yankee I was riding with wanted to talk. He talked about his farm in Illinois and his girl named Belle Anne, who was littler than me. Then he told me about the couple of Negro slaves they'd set free from the mills in New Manchester. The Yankees didn't keep them prisoners the way they had the other New Manchester mill hands. There hadn't been any Negroes working in our mill in Roswell so long as I'd been a bobbin girl there.

My Yankee kept talking, but I didn't hearken much to what he said. My thoughts were on Mama and Jem and what had happened to us. The house we'd been living in long as I could remember was burned down now, and the mill had been set fire to. With the mill not making cloth anymore, what would Mama and the rest of us live on once we were together again? Rosellen's Aunt Marilla lived on Rosellen's earnings, so even if the two of them women had a roof over their heads, how would they buy food?

Tears came to my eyes again and anger to my heart that made me want to pound my fists on the wide blue back of my Yankee soldier. I wanted to somehow get even for Pap's dying and for what was happening to Jem and me.

I looked around to see if I knew anybody nearby. Beside me was a mill girl I knew by sight, but she wasn't anybody I knew truly well. Her face was flour-white, and her lips trembled. Her eyes had a look in them that made me think she didn't even see me, she was so scared.

Finally I asked the Yankee, "Are you takin' us all the way to Indiana?"

He laughed, then said, "No, we don't plan to take you that far. We're only going to Marietta. We got better things to do than haul you Seceshes as freight."

I said, "You won't ever whip us Confederates!"

This made him laugh even more. He answered, "Maybe not, but we'll make a good stab at it. I think probably we will whip you now with the general we got, old Uncle Billy Sherman."

I could have said something to that, but I decided not

to. Let this bluebelly find out for himself how good our soldiers scrapped. I decided not to say another word to him the rest of the way to Marietta. I'd occupy myself instead with plotting how I'd get loose and run home from there.

We got to Marietta, which was thirteen miles from home, fairly soon near sundown and halted in the town square. Yankee officers came riding through and calling out, "Take the mill hands to the Military School. That's where they're to be billeted."

"Billeted"? I didn't know what the word meant, and it scared me. What was going to happen to us there?

We rode away from the town square and before long were at the big brick and wood buildings that were used to train boy soldiers. They were empty now that the students had gone off to war the way Pap and Davey had, so there was room for all of us.

Marietta wasn't burning, though there was some smoke here and there to show that it had been set fire to. I didn't see many folks on the streets as we rode through the town, only Yankee soldiers swarming everywhere as they had in Roswell. They were all around the school, too, waiting for us, which meant that the telegraph between Roswell and Marietta was working.

At the school we were pulled off the horses, and the minute my feet hit the ground, I ran to find Jem and

Rosellen. As I was looking, I heard a bluebelly bellow, "Get the men and boys away from the females."

Get them away? They were going to take my little brother away from me! Swinging my elbows wide, I got through the crowd and found Jem. He was standing with Rosellen, who was holding him and stroking his hair.

I yelled, "Jem, Jem!" Then I ran into Rosellen's embrace, too.

She tried her best to comfort Jem and me by saying over all the yelling and crying and horse noises around us, "Jem, you'll do just fine with the boys here. Don't you fret yourself. We'll be together when we get to Indiana, and then we'll stick together. It's just that they won't put girls and boys together here in this place. Even our own army wouldn't do that with their prisoners. Mr. Catlin, will you come over here and take care of Jemmie Reed, your lap boy?"

Mr. Catlin, a gray-headed man who worked in the carding room with Jem, walked toward us, looking dead weary. He nodded and said, "Sure I will, Rosellen. You bet."

"I thank you."

Rosellen released her grip on Jem and bent to kiss him on the lips. Then he went away with Mr. Catlin, taking the man's hand.

Rosellen told me, "Hannalee, we'll stay together. I'm goin' to tell the Yankees here that I'm your sister-in-law,

Mrs. Davey Reed, and that I'll look out for you here."

I nodded. Then I stood on tiptoe to speak into her ear so no one else could hear, "We'll run away from here soon as we can, but how'll we be able to get Jem to go with us?"

Now she scared me. She reached out, grabbed ahold of me, and shook me hard. Then she hissed at me, "The country between here and Roswell is alive with Yankee soldiers. You wouldn't get a half mile on the way home before they'd catch you."

"But I promised Mama I'd go home!"

Rosellen's eyes were fierce in her sunburned face. She said softly, "Right now, forget that promise. Don't give the bluebellies any trouble. Stay close to me. There's a Yankee officer comin' over to us. Turn around and stand next to me, and don't you say a word."

A tall, skinny bluebelly holding a writing notebook and a pencil in his hand came up to the two of us. He asked Rosellen, "Who'd you be?"

She answered him, "Mrs. Davey Reed, the wife of a Confederate soldier, and this is my husband's little sister, Hannalee Reed. I'm askin' you to keep her and me together so I can look after her. She takes spells of breathin' sickness now and then, and I know how to tend to her. It ain't anythin' catchin'." I gasped at the lie but didn't say a word.

The Yankee looked hard at me, then he said, "Yes, I

hear you mill workers do get lung trouble from breathing lint. All right, we'll put the two of you together in the same room."

Rosellen's voice was thick as she thanked him; for sure, her words had galled her.

Twelve of us were put in a room that held nothing but twelve iron cots with thin mattresses. Four women were from home—Rosellen, me, and two weaver girls—and eight girls were from the mill at New Manchester, a town not far from Roswell. The Yankee cavalry had burned down their mill, too, and fetched the New Manchester mill hands to Marietta by army wagon.

Yankees with muskets stood guard outside the doors and in hallways, and everywhere watched us as we went to eat and wash. We weren't allowed to do anything but walk up and down the halls and lie on our iron beds, looking at the ceilings and thinking of home and our folks. I fretted over Jem and Mama and worried about myself, too.

We lingered in the big school in Marietta for five days. Then on the fifteenth of July the Yankees started collecting us together in front of the school. Us women were brought out first, and after a while a smaller bunch of boys and men came along to join us. When we were all together, a Yankee officer shouted at the top of his lungs, "You rebels will be marched to the train station and will board cars for Nashville, Tennessee, today. Maintain order among yourselves. Make no trouble for us if you value your safety. You will be given rations along the way."

Some of us moaned when we heard this because it meant we'd all be going farther than ever from home. But that was all we could do—moan. Then there was dead quiet as the bluebellies made all eighteen hundred of us Roswell and New Manchester mill hands get into two long lines. As Rosellen and I walked side by side past the school, I saw Yankees with lighted torches start out among the buildings to set them on fire. No Georgia boys would ever learn to be soldiers in this place again. "Curse the race of Yankees!" I said under my breath.

The train station was some distance away, and my feet ached from walking by the time we got there. My head didn't ache from the hot sun, though, because of the kindness of an old lady who came out of a little house on one street we went down. Holding half a dozen calico sunbonnets in her hands, she ran up to the Yankee marching beside me and asked him, "Can I give these to the poor girls? It's so hot today."

When she held the bonnets out to him, he grabbed them, shook the whole bunch to see that there was nothing hidden inside them, then tossed them to me to pass out.

"Thank you," I called out to the old woman, who was now just standing there, staring at us and weeping.

I took a red sunbonnet and put it on, then gave the others to Rosellen. She put on a blue one, tapped one of the girls in front of her on the shoulder and gave her two bonnets, then reached behind her and passed the last two to the mill hands behind us.

The train was waiting for us, and we were ordered up into the cars. Inside were long rows of wooden benches. I sat next to Rosellen by a dirty, streaky window, so I could see the other mill hands board the train, too. I looked hard for Jem, and finally I saw him go by with Mr. Catlin. I opened the window and waved my new red sunbonnet out it, calling, "Jem, Jem Reed! It's Hannalee. I'm up here with Rosellen."

He saw me and shouted back, "Hannalee!" Then he was gone down the line to another car. At the same time a Yankee below me yelled, "Shut that window, girl."

After I did, I turned to Rosellen and asked, "When the train stops somewheres, we can mebbe sneak off and go get Jem?"

She gave me a strange, weary look and shook her head. "No, Hannalee. With all the trouble the Yankees are goin' through with us, do you think they won't put guards inside this car and outside wherever we stop? Don't be feather-headed."

"But as I was leavin' Roswell, I wished upon a crow that I'd get home again, and the crow didn't flap. So I do get my wish."

Rosellen sighed. "That's only a superstition; this is real. The war can't last forever, and when it's over, we'll go home. That's when the Yankees will let us loose."

"Rosellen, mebbe our soldiers will come up to Indiana and save us."

"Mebbe so. I don't know what they'll do." Her voice was broken by a sob, but she continued to talk. "I don't understand how their Gen'ral Sherman got past all our soldiers at Kennesaw Mountain and came to Roswell. Where was our army? Have they all gone to Virginia like your brother Davey? Why didn't our Gen'ral Johnston stop the Yankees? Why are our soldiers still in Atlanta when this is happenin' to us?"

I couldn't answer her because I didn't know why, either. All I could do was sit on the bench and look at the dangling strings of my new sunbonnet. I didn't agree with Rosellen about forgetting my promise to Mama, but I couldn't say so now and rile her. I was still set on keeping my word, though. The persimmon-seed button was deep in my apron pocket. The promise was deep in my mind.

I was glad I sat nearest the window. I planned to keep my eyes on the country we passed through, looking for landmarks. That way I'd be able to find my way when I came back through here again on my way home.

The train jerked forward, and our ride to Indiana began. We knew from the start that it'd be a long one because, as soon as the train got under way, Yankees came through the car carrying cloth sacks with nine days of provisions—corn pone, hard gray biscuits, and tough hog meat.

On and on we went, with the whistle blowing now and then and waking us up if we got to nodding. When we were able to sleep, we did it by leaning against one another with our backs against the rear of the benches. After a day and a night of riding, one of our guards called out, "We're in Tennessee now. Say farewell to Georgia, you women."

Of course, no girl mill hand said "Farewell," but our sour faces must have tickled him, because he laughed at his own joke. As for me, I felt my heart sink just knowing I'd left the only state I'd ever known.

I minded the country we went through heading north and saw little villages set near streams and quiet green forests of pine trees. A girl on the other side of our car said she thought she could make out Lookout Mountain below us, but I didn't want to see any mountains. We'd all been sure the Yankees would be stopped at Kennesaw Mountain, but they weren't. Mountains didn't comfort me. They made me think of what Pap used to say when things went wrong: "Life's lots of times hilly, bumpy, and stumpy."

While the train halted to take on wood in Chattanooga, Tennessee, we were allowed to get off the car and walk around a bit on the train platform. Then we got back aboard, sitting down again just as we had before, and our journey continued.

I watched parts of Tennessee go by my window. We crossed the Tennessee River and after that came farms and rolling land with blue-green grass. I saw fields of growing tobacco and meadows full of wild asters and daisies. Tennessee was pretty enough, but it wasn't home, and every wheel clicking took me farther away.

The next day we stopped in Murfreesboro but weren't allowed off the train. As we pulled out of the station, the guard at one end of our car yelled out to us, "You women are to be billeted in Nashville tonight."

Nashville? Billeted? I pondered the bluebelly's words and I didn't like them. They reminded me of what had happened to us in Marietta, of how we women had been separated from the men and boys. I fretted about Jem, knowing I'd best do something to keep him with us this time.

Finally an idea came to me and I grabbed hold of Rosellen's wrist and said, "Bring your ear over so I can talk into it."

When she did, I whispered my plan. Her eyes got wider, but she didn't say anything. She only reached deep down into the pocket of her mill-worker's apron and took out the little pair of dull scissors the Yankees had let her keep. After Rosellen handed them to me, I turned to the girl across from us and asked if I could borrow the needle and thread I knew she had hidden from the blue-bellies.

When the guards weren't looking, I ducked my head down between the benches, and Rosellen sawed with the scissors at my two long braids of hair. Then, leaning forward, I knotted the braids at the loose ends and sewed them quickly to the sides of the red sunbonnet. After I finished, I put the hat on my head and sat up straight.

Rosellen studied me, then whispered, "Nobody lookin' at you would ever know the braids are on the bonnet, not on you."

Good! I hoped the rest of my plan would go as smoothly. Now I told Rosellen, "Stand up and bend over me like you're starin' out the window." She did, and while she hid me from the guard's sight, I pulled up my skirts, got hold of the drawstrings of my muslin petticoat, and pulled it free. Down it came, and Rosellen picked it up and stuffed it into her deep apron pocket.

After she sat down, I took a deep breath and said, "Now we're ready for Nashville."

The train pulled into the station at dusk. The station was smoky with engine smoke, and that suited me just fine because then it would be hard for the guards to see.

As soon as we got off the train, Rosellen and I called out together, "Jem! Jem Reed!" We reckoned two people calling together would be stronger than just one voice

alone. We were right. Jem heard us and came running
over, grabbing hold of us and hanging on tight.

Rosellen broke his hold on her. As she did, I took the
sunbonnet off my head and jammed it, braids and all, on
his. "Hey, what're you . . . ?" At that very moment
Rosellen put her blue bonnet on me.

We hauled him over into the middle of a group of girls
and women where we couldn't be seen. Then Rosellen
quickly took my petticoat from her apron pocket and
slipped it over Jem's head. I grabbed hold of the strings
and pulled them tight to make a long skirt covering his
pants. The petticoat was so dirty by now that it was more
red-brown than white.

Rosellen said, "Jem, we think the Yankees are fixin' to
take you and the other boys someplace diff'rent than
where we women are bound to. So you're Jemima Reed
now."

Back home nothing would have riled my brother more
than being turned into a girl, but now he took it pretty
well. He opened his mouth to say "No!" but shut it again
fast.

I looked at him. Nobody would ever say he was a
pretty girl, but he could pass for a Jemima. We'd be
together, and that was what mattered.

Just then a Yankee officer on the platform yelled,
"Form into lines, you mill workers. Girls and women
first; men and boys last."

The three of us got into line. As we passed the platform, our names were taken down by a soldier who sat
at a table. He gave us each a number to remember. Rosellen was number thirty-one, I was thirty-two, and Jem
thirty-three.

Finally the Yankee who'd ordered us to form into lines
cried out, "By orders of General Webster, commanding
officer of the Army of the United States in Nashville,
those with numbers from one to three hundred will go
on to Louisville, Kentucky, tonight. The rest will stay in
Nashville."

My hunch had been right. We'd be leaving here right
away. But at least we three would be going on together.

The three hundred of us who were leaving walked
over the railroad tracks to a train that stood puffing steam,
ready to leave. Along the way, I heard Rosellen caution
Jem, "Watch out how you walk. Don't tromp so much
the way a boy does. Walk careful, like me and your
sister."

He told her, "I never had on a skirt 'fore, and in this
bonnet I can't see out the sides."

I asked, "Can you see good out the front?"

"Yep."

"Well, that's all a body needs to see here. There's
nothin' on both sides of us but bluebellies with muskets."

That hushed him up. He walked along with his long
braids swaying.

Chapter Four

Three Ways!

W E RODE ALL THAT NIGHT AND FOR TWO DAYS MORE, sitting and sleeping on the same kind of hard benches as we'd had on the other train. The train stopped a few times to take on more engine wood, and once we were allowed to get out and walk for a spell.

Our train came into Louisville just after daybreak, and we were marched out of the depot the minute we got off of the cars. We walked between big brick and cast-iron buildings, but it was so early that nobody else was up and around as yet.

We came to the Ohio River just north of the city. Never in my life had I seen so much water in one time. This broad, slow-moving river made Vickerys' Creek look like nothing at all. Boats, paddle-wheel steamers, and steamboats were moving up and down the river. Jem, Rosellen, and I stood on the shore and stared and stared across it to the other side.

Jem asked, "That's Indiana over there, huh?"

"That's right," agreed Rosellen.

He asked, "If they fetched us here, do they expect us to swim over the water?"

"I don't know. Mebbe they just want us to see how big their river is. We'll find out what the Yankees want soon enough. They're all around us, thick as fleas."

Suddenly an army wagon pulled up near to us, and some soldiers got down from it and lifted wooden boxes out of the back. Then an officer yelled, "You Georgia people, take off your boots and leave them here on the bank. Make it fast, and remember where they are."

Take off our boots? Although the order didn't seem to make much sense, we all obeyed. I bent over, unlaced mine, and took them off. Soon there were three hundred pairs standing in the grass.

Now the same officer shouted, "File by the boxes and get a bar of soap. Go down into the water and wash yourselves and your clothing. Then come back and get your boots on."

I looked at Jem, then at Rosellen. She whispered to me, "We'll stay together in the water. Wash the bonnets and put them right back on your heads. When you wash your hair, I'll stand over you so nobody will see you both have short hair."

I asked, "What about you? Once you wash, they'll see your head's gold-colored."

"It don't matter that they see it here. I don't care. Come on now. Get the soap."

In spite of its being July, that river water was cold. We three shivered as we got down into it, soaped our dresses and ourselves, then ducked all the way under, washing our hair. Jem and I took off our sunbonnets, washed our heads, and then put the hats back on again with nobody being the wiser. Jem's braids stayed on despite the washing because I'd stitched them as good and strong as I was able.

Once we were all finished and back on shore, the bluebellies marched us to a big wood building. It looked like the warehouse at our mill back home, but this one smelled bad of tar and coal oil. I reckoned that was what had been stored here. The light was dim and the building damp. Inside, the Yankees handed out blankets to us and fed us hot soup and white bread. Even if they were Yankee victuals, they were mighty welcome.

After we ate, we settled down on the floor around the edges of that big room and I noticed that other folks beside soldiers began to come inside—both men and la-dies. Most of them were old and wore gray and black clothing. Some of the men wore black bands on their sleeves. A few women carried baskets over their arms.

A gentle-faced lady, dressed in dark gray from head to toe, came up to us three. She gave us each a hair comb and a ripe red plum from her basket.

Rosellen thanked her kindly for the three of us, then asked, "Ma'am, who would you be?"

"My name doesn't matter, child. I'm from one of the

churches here in Louisville. So are the others here. The men are ministers and pastors."

When Jem said, "We go to church in Georgia," the lady smiled.

Now Rosellen asked, "What'll they do with us? Do you know?"

The woman nodded. "I believe so. General Webster has sent you here to our Provost Marshal, Captain James. He has put advertisements in the newspapers regarding you mill workers. I saw one this morning."

Rosellen asked, "They were about us?"

"Yes, they were."

"What do they say?"

"Just a moment, my girl. The lady who came here with me, I believe, has a copy of the morning paper with her. Amelia, would you come over here, please."

Amelia, who was older than the other woman and dressed in black cloth that rustled when she walked, came over to us. When the lady in gray asked about the paper, she took a folded one from her basket, opened it, and found the right page, then read out loud to us:

"NOTICE: Families residing in the city or country wishing seamstresses or servants can be suited by applying at the refugee headquarters on Broadway between Ninth and Tenth. This is sanctioned by Capt. James, Provost Marshal."

I looked at Rosellen, and she stared back at me. Then she told the ladies, "We're mill hands, not servants. I'm a drawin' girl. I'm a skilled worker, not a seamstress."

I added, "I don't sew good, either. I'm a bobbin girl."

"And what about you, child?" the lady named Amelia asked Jem.

"I'm a lap b . . ." he started, but caught himself in time and finished with "girl."

"Well, my girl, you may end up as servants here in Kentucky. You factory people are traitors after all, aren't you? Should traitors be choosers?" The woman in black sniffed, then up and left like she didn't want to have any part of the three of us from Roswell.

The other woman stayed behind just long enough to say, "Put your trust in Providence, children. The Lord will see to it that you are all placed in proper places. Kentucky has far too few hands to do her work now that her able-bodied men have gone to war and our blessed President Lincoln has mercifully given the black slaves their freedom. You will all find employment to occupy your hands."

Jem growled, "I don't want to work for Yankees."

This made the woman frown. She told Jem, "My girl, if you do not work, you shall very likely not have food to eat. Why should you eat if you do not work?"

Jem flared at her, "We didn't want to come up here. We got hauled off by your bluebelly soldiers!"

Now the lady was mad as hops. She said, "You were brought here to bring this dreadful war to an end more swiftly. You are traitors to the Union. If you do not work, you may very likely go to prison. I shall not speak further to you. I hope the people who hire you will guide you in wisdom as well as keep your hands, souls, and consciences free of the devil's temptations. And don't use the word 'bluebelly.' It is coarse and vulgar to the extreme!" And off she sailed, too.

Bad as I wanted it, I threw my plum into a corner. A second later, so did Jem. Not Rosellen, though. As she looked after the two women, she slowly ate her plum. Then she began to comb the snarls out of her long hair with the comb the Yankee lady had given her.

Not long after, a soldier came through with a pencil and a notebook. He asked our names and what kind of work we'd done in our mill. He wrote down what we'd done after our names. Then he said, "When you hear 'weaver' or 'spinner' or 'drawing girl' called out, go to the part of the building you are told to."

Rosellen asked him, "What about these two young 'uns? They're a bobbin girl and a lap girl."

"They stay here where they are unless those jobs are asked for, too. The owners and managers of cloth mills are coming here from miles around to hire skilled workers. I guess you can make Union blue as well as Confederate gray, can't you, Goldilocks?" He reached out and caught hold of a lock of Rosellen's hair.

She let him touch it, but when he let it go, she tossed it back behind her head and leaned against the wall so he couldn't grab it again.

Once he'd gone on to some other mill hands nearby, I cried, "Oh, Rosellen!"

She said sharply, "Hush, Hannalee. Don't let 'em see you're scared."

"I *am* scared! They'll split us up."

She nodded. "Mebbe so, but if they do, what can we do about it? Do what they tell you to. Wait till the war's over and done with. They've got the upper hand now."

"Not on me, they haven't. No matter where they take me, I'm goin' to run away home."

"Me, too," came from Jem. "Me and Hannalee'll run away back home. How about you, Rosellen?"

"I been thinkin' a lot on our way up here. I'm goin' to see which way the cat jumps before I do anythin' at all."

"Rosellen, you'd work for *Yankees?*"

She nodded slowly. "You heard what that old lady told us. I'd work for Yankees before I'd go to one of their jails. I think you'd best bear that in mind, too. That train ride was like a jail on wheels, and remember how bad *it* was. Just think what a real bluebelly prison would be like."

I did think, and so did Jem, and I could tell from his face he didn't like what he was remembering, either.

*   *   *

That afternoon a bunch of men in business clothes came into the building and stood by the doors. A Yankee officer got up on a pile of empty barrels and shouted out for everybody to be quiet. Then he said, "Those among you who are drawing girls come to the table by the doors. The rest of you stay where you are."

That meant Rosellen. I watched her get up, smooth down her skirts, and shake back her long hair. She looked down at Jem and me, and I could see she was biting at her lower lip, trying not to cry. She told us, "If somebody takes me, I'll try to see to it that he hires both of you, too, so we can be together." Then, walking fast, she left us and went to stand with the group of men and girls gathering at the table where some soldiers sat.

Jem moved closer to me, and we watched as the men from the Northern mills began to talk with the Georgia people. Two of them were talking to Rosellen. One was a tall, wide-bodied old man in a fawn-colored coat and a brown beaver hat. The other was tall, slender, and young. His hair was the color of fall leaves, and he was dressed all in pale gray. The both of them bent their heads to listen to Rosellen. Then I saw them nod and go on to the girl standing next to her.

Jem said sadly, "Them two are goin' to take Rosellen away with 'em." Though I agreed with him, I didn't say anything.

We were right. A little later the two men went up to

the officer at a table. Nine women and girls trailed behind them, and one of them was Rosellen.

The older man talked to the officer, who then spoke to each of the womenfolks and wrote something down. When he had finished, he gave the old man a piece of paper, nodded, and smiled. He signaled to the guards on each side of the door to let the two men and the nine women out.

"*Rosellen!*" Jem was up in a flash and running over the floor. I leaped up, too, and ran after him. We both caught hold of Rosellen and held her tight.

I asked, "Where are you goin'? Aren't we comin', too?"

"No, you can't come. They said that they won't hire you and Jem, because they don't need bobbin girls right now. I'm going to Indiana—to Cannelton—across the Ohio River."

Over the river? Indiana? Would Jem and I go to Indiana, too? Would we at least be able to stay in the same state together?

Rosellen bent and kissed each of us, then a Yankee guard pulled us away and she went out the door—the last of the nine to leave.

Jem and I slept real close together that night, wrapped up in Yankee blankets on the hard floor. The next morning after breakfast more Northern folks came to look us over. A tall, thin lady dressed in brown with a tan and green shawl over her shoulders was brought over to us by one of the preachers.

In a twanging voice she told us, "I'm here looking for nimble-fingered girls to trim bonnets in my shop. Do you girls sew?"

I told her truthfully, "No, ma'am. I wasn't ever a good sewer, and my little sister don't sew so good, either."

"Perhaps you can learn. Let me see your hands. I'm looking for small fingers."

When we held our hands out to her, she grabbed hold of them and twisted, then bent our fingers. She soon let go of my hands, but she kept hold of Jem's, who had long fingers like Pap's.

"I'll take this smaller girl," she told the preacher next to her. To Jem she said, "What is your name, little girl?"

Being called a "girl" again was one time too many for Jem. He did the last thing in the world I had wanted him to do. He jerked off the red sunbonnet and, braids flying, threw it onto the floor, then undid the drawstrings to my petticoat and let it fall. He cried out, "I'm *Jem* Reed! I'm not a girl! I won't sew bonnets for anybody anywhere."

The preacher just stared at him and me and steered the surprised-looking lady away with a hand under her elbow.

"Oh, Jem," I said softly. I longed to stamp and yell, but I was quiet. He'd done damage to us, and that was that. What would happen to us now that the Yankees knew he was a boy?

After a time a brown-bearded man in black boots and rough-looking clothes came clumping up to us. He stood over us, staring down hard at Jem. Finally he said, "You, boy! I got to find a hired boy on my farm to take the place of the one that enlisted in the army last week. Have you ever pitched hay, weeded tobacco, or milked a cow? Stand up and answer me so I see you understand what I'm sayin' to ya."

Jem stood up and said, "No, I never have done them things."

"Well, they don't take much thinkin' or trainin'. You can learn. You're big enough for what I want. I'll take ya."

"Will you take my sister, too?"

The farmer looked down his thick nose at me and shook his head. "No, I don't need your sis. I got daughters and a wife to do the work womenfolks do. You come on now!" He grabbed Jem by the left arm and hauled him to the table by the door.

Jem was leaving me! I was going to be alone—all *alone* here now in this big building. Where was he going? How would I find him? I knew the Yankee officer would never tell me even if I asked him kindly. I kept my eyes on Jem, wishing, hoping, begging him to come back and tell me where he was going.

He did! He stood for a minute with the farmer while his name was taken down. Then Jem said something to the man and came racing back to me to hug me hard.

Talking fast, he said, "His name's Hopkins, Rufus Hopkins. He lives close to Hartford. That's here in Kentucky. Good-bye, Hannalee. I love you!"

Then he walked slowly back to the farmer, leaving me sitting on the floor with my eyes so full of tears I couldn't see him go out the door. Why hadn't I thought to tell him I loved him, too, and say, "God bless you, Jemmie Reed!"

Chapter Five

The Head-Bump Yankee and His Missus

Now I was all alone. I sat curled up in my blanket, sorrowing and waiting until dark to cry so the Yankees couldn't see my tears. I mourned the end of my hopes that Rosellen, Jem, and I would be together here in the North. We didn't even stay two together.

At the end of that long day, a small man and a tiny little woman came over to me. The woman looked me over from head to foot, then said, "Take off your bonnet so I can see the shape of your skull, girl."

Folks had asked me to take off the bonnet a few times that day, but never because of my skull. They had all just wanted to get a good view of me. No one had taken to my shaggy-headed, short-haired looks, and they had all muttered and gone off to look at other mill hands more handsome than I was.

I sighed and took off the blue bonnet again, thinking of the braids that were on the floor sewed to Jem's red hat. A lot of good cutting my braids off had done us!

When I got my bonnet off, the man came up to me

and felt all over my head as though he was expecting me to have louse nits in my hair. I longed to tromp on his toes, but didn't dare. I'd seen a mill girl slap someone that day who'd pinched her arm to see how strong she was. She was dragged out by bluebelly guards right off, and she never came back inside.

The man feeling my head told the woman in a wheezing voice, "Lucy May, this one doesn't have the bumps of a liar or a lazybones or a thief. She looks strong enough to work in the house."

The woman ordered me, "Tell me your name."

"Hannalee Reed."

"Folks cut off their hair because of fevers. Why is your hair cut off? Are you sick? Have you had a fever recently?"

"No, ma'am," I replied and told her what I'd done to save Jem.

She said, "So that's why. At least you aren't sickly. It was simple deceit on your part." She sighed. "We are Mr. and Mrs. James Fletcher. We live here in Louisville. My husband studies phrenology. He has not liked the skulls of others here, but he likes yours." She looked at me closely, then continued. "We need a servant girl to do the house chores. Even if you are a little Dixie rebel who probably hasn't got any more manners than a calf at a milk pail, we will take you. Perhaps we can teach you a thing or two. Come along with us now."

Walking behind them, carrying Jem's and my sunbonnets plus the food sack the Yankees had given me on the train ride from Georgia, I started getting mad. What right did these two Yankees have to feel my head to make sure I didn't have any badness inside me? There wasn't any laziness or meanness in any of us Reeds. We worked hard in the mill and tended to our own business. It took Yankees to think that I might be bad. They treated us Georgia folks like we were slaves—like they owned us and we had no say over anything at all. Well, I hated the whole devil race of bluebellies! I glared as hard as I could at the soldier who took down my name and gave the Fletchers a paper releasing me to them, but he didn't even look up at me. The Fletchers didn't see my face, either.

The three of us walked outside, and Miz Fletcher said, "We shall walk, James. The constitutional will benefit us. Hannalee, you had best put on that sunbonnet so nobody will see what's been done to your hair. You'll wear a servant girl's cap in our house." After walking a few steps, Miz Fletcher paused with one finger to her lips. Then she said to me, "I don't fancy your name. Hannalee is too common-sounding. I will change it to something more elegant. James, what about Carabelle? I like it. That is what we shall call you."

Carabelle! I'd never heard such a name in my whole life.

The Fletcher house was a distance away from the building where we had been held prisoners. It was a pretty little brick house on the edge of the town. By looking out the side of the Fletchers' front porch I could just see the Ohio River, red in the sunset.

There was a breeze off the river, but the house was hot as blue blazes inside. Mr. Fletcher led me upstairs to a little room under the roof. Even with the one little window open, it was so hot inside there that I had to gasp for breath. In winter it'd most likely be cold as dying.

I didn't get any supper that night, and after a sleepless night Miz Fletcher called me down early and fed me some mush in the kitchen. Then she took me onto the back porch and gave me a gray cotton dress, a white apron, and a white cap. She told me, "This is a maid's outfit. The last girl we had wore it. You look the proper size for it."

As I took the things, I asked, "What happened to her, Miz Fletcher?"

"She died last month. She was an orphan girl. She got galloping pneumonia and it took her fast."

Galloping pneumonia! I sighed. It didn't gladden me to wear a dead girl's clothes, but then I didn't have a choice, and I didn't think that pneumonia was catching like smallpox and consumption.

The clothes did fit me good enough, and after I'd put them on, Miz Fletcher told me what I was to do. Just hearing her tell all the chores, ticking them off on her fingers, made me feel weary to the bone already. And I was to be paid only three dollars a month, and room and board. I got *eight* dollars a month working at the mill back home. But Miz Fletcher said that the dead orphan girl got three dollars and that the army officer who gave the Fletchers my release papers had told them it was downright handsome.

Doing all those chores was lots worse than hearing about them. First I scrubbed the floors on my hands and knees with a stiff brush. Then I beat the rugs with a rug beater outside on the Fletchers' clothesline. I polished their furniture with neat's-foot oil and dusted with a feather duster. I was in every room in that house except their bedroom, which Miz Fletcher tidied herself. She wouldn't let me set foot inside it, and I was just as glad; it was one room I wouldn't have to clean.

Although Miz Fletcher did the cooking, I was in the kitchen plenty. I boiled the wash in big copper boilers on the red-hot stove. When the stove cooled down, I blackened it with stove polish and shined up the nickel plate on it. I ironed the clothes after they dried, and when I scorched a petticoat with a too-hot iron, Miz Fletcher rapped me on the head with a wood cooking spoon.

The next day was pretty much the same, though I did different chores. I worked from the minute I came down to the minute she sent me up to bed.

I hated it there. The Fletchers saw me only as a servant slaving away. Though sometimes Mr. Fletcher gave me a smile, Miz Fletcher didn't talk to me at all except to tell me what I had to do next.

One afternoon during my second week with the Fletchers, Miz Fletcher told me to do the parlor with more than usual care because she was having some company. While I dusted every little-bitty thing in the room, she put garden flowers in the vases. When everything was clean, she went up to her bedroom and came back with a framed photograph and set it in the middle of the mantel.

The picture was of a young man who looked a little like Mr. Fletcher, but younger. He had dark hair and sideburns and was dressed in a Yankee soldier's uniform. Miz Fletcher sighed deep as she looked at him. Then she took some shiny black cloth flowers and leaves out of her lace apron pocket and put them around the sides and top of the picture. When she finished, she stood back to look at it.

I asked, "Who'd that be, ma'am?"

"Our only boy, Charlie. I want my lady guests to see how handsome he was. Some of them have never seen him. I keep Charlie's picture in our room, so it's the first thing I see in the morning and the last thing at night before I fall asleep. He was killed at Gettysburg."

Suddenly she turned her head and gave me a wicked look. She snapped, "Go about your work. I didn't fetch him down to be stared at by the likes of you. If it wasn't for you rebels starting the war, our Charlie would still be with us!"

I had it on the tip of my tongue to say that if it hadn't been for Yankees wanting to fight to keep us in their Union, Pap would have stayed home and most likely been alive now. I kept quiet, though it galled me.

Miz Fletcher asked me, "I never asked you before— is any of your family in the Confederate Army? Did anyone fight at Gettysburg?"

I nodded. "Yes'm. My pap and my brother Davey were there at Gettysburg. Pap's dead now because of the war, but Davey's somewheres in Virginia with our army. I'm mighty proud of Davey Reed!"

Oh, how Miz Fletcher goggled her eyes at me and screeched, "May curses rain down on his damnable rebel head!" She pointed a trembling finger at me. "If it wasn't for our other servant girl dying and our not being able to get anyone else, I wouldn't have you here. Do you think I relish having a dirty little traitor in my house? And now I find you proud of being a rebel and having a rebel soldier for a brother. You miserable little maw-mouth girl!"

Mawmouth! I hated that word more than any other that she could call me.

"Get out to the kitchen and stay out there. I don't want my guests to have to look at your face."

*   *   *

After that afternoon, things went from bad to lots worse between her and me. She only talked to me to scold me for bad work, and I often caught her glaring at me. The Fletchers never took me anyplace but to their church, and when Miz Fletcher spoke about me to the church folks she knew, she called me "the ignorant, wretched, unlettered Georgia mill girl James and I have taken in out of the goodness of our hearts."

Oh, how I hated her and her house! I dreamed at night of home and of our old house. Sometimes I could even smell Pap's roses at the back door. When I ate the good Yankee food, I thought of how Mama and Rosellen's aunt were eating and felt truly guilty. Seeing how good the Northerners lived made me realize that the war wasn't hurting them anywhere near as bad as it was hurting us Confederates.

Mr. Fletcher treated me better than his wife did. He worked as a bank clerk during the day, so I didn't see him too often. But sometimes when he was at home, he'd talk to me while I worked.

One afternoon toward the middle of August, he was reckoning up numbers on some papers in the dining room while I polished the furniture. When he looked up from his work, I told him, "Mr. Fletcher, I come up here to Louisville with my little brother, Jem, and a girl we used to know. She went to work in Indiana at a place called Cannelton. Do you know where that is?"

"Of course, Carabelle. It's not too far from here."

I nodded. Good, Rosellen was nearby. Then I went on polishing until he asked me, as I reckoned he would, "Where's your brother?"

"Near Hartford. A farmer who wanted a hired boy took him there the day before you folks came for me. Where's that?"

"Some eighty or so miles to the west."

I thanked him kindly for the information, but wasn't happy about it. Jem was a far piece from me.

Mr. Fletcher got up from his chair and touched me on the shoulder, saying, "You're a serious child. I think you're a good girl and responsible, too. I wish my wife didn't feel so strongly against you because our son was killed. It isn't your fault your brother's a Southern soldier. You must miss your family a great deal."

I felt like busting out into tears at the first kind word I'd had in weeks, but I held it all in. I did say, "I truly do miss my kin. Mama was going to have a baby 'fore long. Pap died of fever in Virginia early this year. Because of the new baby comin', Mama wasn't workin' in the mill, so the soldiers didn't take her away when they took Jem and me and the others."

"Have you always been mill hands?"

"Pap and Mama were ever since they were my age. Us Reeds have been makin' cotton cloth for a long time. We worked for every cent we ever got, and when the war come, the menfolks went off to it and Jem and me worked on." I sighed. "I wish the war had never happened at all."

"So do I, Carabelle." He sighed deeply, too, and I knew he was thinking of his boy. Then he said, "I wish slavery had never existed in this country."

I nodded and told him, "I want you to know that none of us Reeds ever owned a black slave. Sometimes I saw the millowners' slaves and the slaves who come to Roswell from the plantations around us, but I don't recall ever passin' two words with one of them. You know, it don't seem right to me that folks like us Reeds should have such hard times now when we never had slaves. We did all our work ourselves. We don't hold with slavery. Pap wanted all the slaves set free everywhere. He didn't think it was right that a man should own another man. He used to say he wasn't the only Southerner who favored the idea of freedom for slaves."

Mr. Fletcher nodded, too. "He *wasn't* the only one. It's a pity things turned out this way for all of us. Civil war's the worst kind of war at all. But it can't last forever. I keep telling myself and my wife that."

I asked, "Do you hear when there are battles fought? There ought to be news about 'em in the newspapers you read at night."

"There is. That's about all the news there is nowadays —news about battles and skirmishes and lists of the dead and wounded. It doesn't make for good reading. There's been some news lately from Georgia. A battle was fought at Peachtree Creek late last month, and the Union forces won. Atlanta is under siege by our troops. So far the city is holding out, but it can't for long." He would have said more, but just then we heard Miz Fletcher hollering "Carabelle" from the kitchen.

As I left to see what Miz Fletcher wanted from me now, I told myself that I just had to do something about the Fletchers. Even if he was nice for a Yankee, she was a mean-natured female. She was going to make a crazy-mad person out of me if I stayed here much longer. I had to get away from the Fletcher house, and I had to do it fast.

Chapter Six

Twelve Men from Missouri

MY CHANCE CAME ON A HOT NIGHT LATE IN AUGUST, sometime after Mr. Fletcher had paid me my three dollars for the month. I kept the Yankee paper money deep in the apron pocket of my maid's uniform next to Mama's persimmon-seed button.

That day was a bad one because Miz Fletcher was so close after me with orders that I could hardly call my soul my own. She had me scour all her griddles and skillets and the rest of the iron pots till my fingers were bloody. Then, in the full heat of the day, she made me wallop the daylights out of six dirty old rag rugs I dragged down from the attic. By sundown I was so weary of Miz Fletcher that I wished I had wings to fly away from her.

And by luck that was the very day I got to sprout them, too. That night both Fletchers went out together for the first time. They were going to a special talk on the U.S. Sanitary Commission, which did the Union Army nursing. Hearing this talk was important to them, so they felt they could go even if they were still in mourning.

After supper Miz Fletcher ordered me up to my room, and to my surprise she came upstairs after me. When I went inside and shut my door, I heard a clicking sound as the key she'd had in her hand all the way up the steps was turned in my keyhole.

By all the Holy Hokies, she'd locked me in!

I didn't let out one yelp. Instead, I listened at the door to hear her going downstairs again. Then I went to my little window, looked out, and, by craning my neck, saw them leave the house together.

The minute the Fletchers were out of sight, I changed into my own clothes. I tied my old boots around my neck and stuffed both sunbonnets and my money into my dress front. Then I got the bits of bread and cheese I'd been saving up for days and put them into the cloth food sack I kept from the train ride north. After tying the strings of the sack around my neck, I sat down in front of the window and waited for the sun to set.

Once it grew dark, I squeezed through the window and crawled out onto the steep shingle roof. The Fletchers had probably counted on my being too scared to go out on it, or they'd thought I was too bulky to get through the window—but either way they were wrong. I was brave enough, and I was skinny enough.

I slowly worked my way around to the side of the house where there was a good, strong trellis full of honeysuckle. It'd hold my weight, I was sure.

It didn't take me long to climb down the trellis into the flower garden below. A minute later I was through the back gate into the alley and heading down another street, going west. Nobody saw me leave except a neighbor's big white tomcat. I was scared, but I was free of the Fletchers.

What should I do now? I leaned against a brick wall to think and catch my breath. My heart was pounding hard. I couldn't swim the Ohio River to get to Rosellen, and I was scared to try riding over it in a boat. So that left Hartford, where Jem was. The best thing was to go there and look for him.

I was scared half to death starting out all alone for a place I'd never been to and hardly knew the location of. But with my hand over Mama's persimmon-seed button for courage, I knew that I'd have to find the heart in me to do it. No matter what, I had to find Jem. And once I did, I wouldn't be alone anymore.

That night I slept in a woodshed in Louisville. Early the next morning I started walking again. A man came hurrying by, and I asked him which road I needed to take to get to Hartford. I reckoned that because he was in a hurry he wouldn't take the time to stop and ask why a girl was traveling there alone. I figured right—he told me the road, and on he went.

A piece down the road I came across an empty whiskey bottle somebody had tossed away. I washed it out at a street pump, filled it with water, and put it in my food sack. I was glad to have something to drink, because August was as hot in Kentucky as it was in Georgia, and I got heated just walking slowly along the side of the road.

Now and then wagons full of Yankee soldiers passed by just a few feet from me. The men would call out, joshing me, a girl walking alone. I didn't like that. They were taking too much notice of me. I had to do something about it, and when a boy my size walked past me, he gave me an idea. If I got myself up to look like a boy, people wouldn't pay any attention to me at all. But how could I do that?

Some miles out of Louisville, on a stretch of road with only a few houses on it, I spied what I needed to change me into a boy. I left the road, ducked under a split-rail fence, and crossed the pasture. Hiding behind some bushes, I waited until a woman and a girl finished hanging up the Monday wash and went back into their whitewashed house. Then I ran over and grabbed down the boy's blue cotton shirt and overalls they'd just put on the washing line. I raced back to the bushes with them and sat there for a while shivering like a rabbit the dogs hadn't caught up to yet. When my heart finally calmed down, I took off my sunbonnet and dress and put on the wet shirt and overalls. They fit me all right and, hot as it was, they'd soon dry on me.

To make up for my stealing, I hung my calico dress out on top of the bushes so the folks I stole from would be sure to see it. Then I jerked the braids off the red sunbonnet, hid them in an animal hole under the bushes, and hung both sunbonnets alongside the dress.

Hannalee Reed had walked off the road. Hannibal Reed walked back onto it—with his ma's persimmon seed in one pants pocket and the paper money in the other.

I walked and walked until sunset. That night I slept under the dogtrot walk of a house. I didn't want to sleep where it was truly wild because I was scared of bears and snakes. In the morning I was on my way to Jem again. I had my story ready in case I had to talk to somebody. I was an orphan from Louisville being sent away by a cruel-natured uncle to a kind aunt who lived in Hartford. If someone asked what side my family favored in the war, I'd say they had men serving on both the Union and Confederate sides. Mr. Fletcher had told me that lots of Kentuckians were in the Confederate Army.

That day I ran into a piece of good luck. A man driving a wagon pulled by an old sorrel mare offered me a ride. I took it and told him my new name and my story. He seemed to believe me and didn't ask me any questions.

After a time he told me, "I don't go all the way to Hartford. I'm going to another town some miles past it to the south. I'll take you to the crossroads for Hartford and set you down there. How's that, young man?"

"That'd suit me just fine. Thank you."

We didn't talk much along the way, which pleased me. The less I said, the less I was likely to muddy up my story.

Near sundown he set me down at a crossroads and went off at a trot. The roads were deserted, and there were no houses or barns in sight.

After I ate the last of my food, I had to find some place near people to spend the night. A barn or woodshed or even a chicken coop was what I hoped for. After walking over two hills, I finally found a little log house down in a hollow. From where I stood, I could hear a dog barking, so I didn't go nearer. I found a beech tree that stood at the edge of a grove of trees not too far from the house. The tree had a comfortable big crotch to lie down in, so I climbed up into it, hoping I wouldn't fall out during the night.

I fell asleep thinking of Pap, wondering if he could see where I was now. What would he think of my idea to find Jem and take him away home to Georgia with me? I thought Pap would have favored the idea.

I didn't know what time of night it was when I was awakened by noises from below my tree. They were cavalry sounds—horses snorting softly, the clink of metal on the bridles, and the creaking of leather. Men were talking quietly, but I couldn't make out what they said.

Suddenly one of them spoke louder and I heard, "Whoever they are down there, they sure don't expect anything to happen."

A second, deeper voice chuckled and added, "Do you expect they're Confederates or Yankees, Bill?"

"It don't matter," came the first voice. "We got our

needs, and that comes first. Let's get on with it. Come on, men."

I didn't move. I tried not to breathe. There was enough moonlight for me to see twelve men riding up to the house at a walk. The dog began to bark from inside it. Three riders got off their horses and walked up to the door. They were wearing ghost-white duster coats that came down almost to their heels and dark-colored felt hats. One of them had a pistol.

Bang! The man shot the latch of the front door. Then all three men booted the door open, jumped aside, and shot the big white dog that ran out. Yelling and screaming came from inside, and very soon a man, a woman, and two little kids came out of the house with their hands up in the air. The men still on horseback had taken muskets out of their saddle scabbards and now trained them on the family.

One rider shouted out, "We come for your valuables —money and jewelry! I mean bus'ness, or my name ain't William Quantrill of Missouri!"

"Quantrill?" cried the woman, clutching at her chest.

Her husband limped forward and tried to say something, but was knocked to the ground by two of the men on foot. As he lay on the ground, he shouted out, "We ain' . . . ," but before he could get any more words out of his mouth, one of the riders shot him in the chest.

The fear and horror of it were too much, and I let out

a yelp. My cry pierced the sudden quiet, and at once one of the riders came trotting over to my beech tree, pistol raised upward. He called out, "Who the devil's up there?"

So scared my teeth rattled, I cried, "Me! I'm named Hannibal Reed."

"Well, get on down or I'll set fire to this tree and roast you alive."

I don't recall how I got down, but I did. I stood on the ground beside the horseman, who looked down at me and said, "It's a shirttail boy. Do you want to see him, Bill, or should I get shed of him right here on the spot?"

Shoot me? I knew that that was what he meant, and I froze.

A call came, "Bring him over here."

The woman was kneeling over her husband, crying, and I walked over to her. One of Quantrill's men had gone inside the house and now came out with a lit kerosene lamp. A second man walked past me with two pillowcases stuffed with things from the house. The man with the lamp brought it over and held it so close to me that I could smell its smoking wick. His other hand held a big horse pistol to the side of my neck.

I stared at Quantrill, a tall, tow-headed man with a thin face and narrow lips. He asked me, "Are you related to these folks here?"

"No, sir. I'm on my way to my aunt in Hartford and I got lost. When it got dark, I went up a tree for the night.

I'm an orphan." I was so scared that I shook as I spoke.

Quantrill asked me, "Can you give me one good reason why I shouldn't shoot you, too?"

I couldn't make my mind think, let alone make up any more lies. Then all at once I thought of what had happened to me in Roswell and in Louisville and decided I'd tell him the truth. "I'm from Georgia," I told him, "not from Kentucky at all. I'm a mill worker. I'm sorry I told you a lie just now. I ain't got any kin in Hartford. The Yankees captured me in Roswell, Georgia, and fetched me and other mill hands all the way to Louisville to work for 'em or go to jail. I ran away from the people I worked for. I'm headed back home to Georgia, and I'm truly lost. I want to go home, but I don't know the way. I'm a Confederate. My brother's in the army in Virginia. I'd rather be shot right now than go back to the people I worked for in Louisville. But if you do shoot me, you won't be shootin' any Yankee boy. And that is a true fact!"

I'd babbled to him like a crazy person, but it'd been all I could think of to say to his question.

For a long time he was quiet, then he began to laugh. He laughed and laughed. Pretty soon his men joined in. When they finally stopped, Quantrill told me, "No, I won't shoot you, and neither will anybody else. I never heard anything the likes of what you just told me. I didn't know that any Georgia mill hands were taken to the

North." He leaned toward me in his saddle. "But you'll never get to Georgia the way you're going. You're headed west, not south, boy." He opened his duster to show me the red shirt he wore and went on talking. "I'm called a guerrilla now, but I used to be an officer in the Confederate Army. Even then I wore a red shirt. When you grow up and have grandkids, you tell 'em you saw William Quantrill and that he spared your life because you're a true Southern lad. If you were old enough, you'd be a real fire-eater in any man's army!"

Then he rose up in his stirrups and shouted, "All right, men, we're done here. Fire the house! Then let's be on our way before any bluebelly cavalry sees the fire and comes after us. There are patrols all over."

The man with the lamp threw it through the open door, and flames jumped up at once. As soon as the bushwhackers saw the fire catch, they rode away from the house, leaving behind the dead man, his red-haired, pale wife, their two little yellow-headed boys, and me.

I went up to the woman, who was sitting on the ground rocking back and forth, and asked if I could be of help.

She looked at me and said with anger, "That was that Missouri devil Quantrill. My man, Clem, wouldn't leave here when the neighbors told us Yankee cavalry was huntin' that bushwhacker Quantrill in these parts. We're for the South. Clem had a bad leg, or he'd be in the

Confederate Army right now. Clem said Quantrill was a Confederate officer and wouldn't harm a hair on our heads because we're Southern, too. I wish the Yankees'd catch them murderin' devils and hang all of 'em!" Then she buried her face in her arms and went on rocking. She didn't speak to me again.

Seeing the misery he had brought to innocent people, I cussed Quantrill. So long as I lived, I'd remember him for his robbing and murdering. He wasn't any true Confederate. He was a crazy man, only out for himself.

And I cursed the war for the wicked, devilish thing it was. It was bad enough for armed soldiers to be killed, but what about common folks? They didn't even shoulder a musket, yet bad things happened to them in their own homes all the same.

I didn't know how to help this grieving family any. All I could do was to kiss the crying boys on top of their heads and hug the rocking woman. Then I left her and the burning house.

When I was out of their sight, I all at once got sick. I leaned against a tree and threw up till I ached in my stomach. I'd been scared half out of my head by Quantrill, and my heart hurt for the woman and her kids. I wished I could have left something for them, but I didn't have anything to give. Nor could I bring the man back to life or build them a new cabin.

After a time I felt better and walked on. I came to a

thicket of trees growing along the side of a little stream. The sound of the fast-running water reminded me how thirsty I was, so I went down to the stream, pushing my way through the thicket, and lay down to wash out my mouth and drink.

I was cupping my hands to drink when I heard hoof-beats coming toward me. *Horses!* Was it Quantrill again? Or Yankee cavalry?

I stayed where I was on my belly, froze up like a possum cornered by a dog, praying I wouldn't be seen. The horses were walking slowly, and I caught a glimpse of sabers swinging from saddles. They were Yankee horse soldiers coming down from the other side of the stream. From the quiet and slow way they rode, I was positive they were out hunting—hunting Quantrill.

They came through the water single file, with the first one passing so close to me I could hear both the horse's and man's breathing. The horse snuffled, and the rider hushed him with "It's all right, Brutus. There's nothing there."

Thank goodness I was hidden by the bushes! I held my breath and didn't move a muscle as some twenty riders passed by in the dark. When they were gone and I couldn't hear them anymore, I poured cold water over my head to calm myself down. Then I took another drink and lay on my back, looking up at the stars and waiting for my heart to stop its pounding.

Running into this Yankee cavalry made me do some hard thinking. I cursed that evil bushwhacker again. Quantrill had brought a swarm of Yankees down on *my* head as well as his own. The roads would be full of bluebellies out searching for him, and I was almost as scared of being caught by them as I had been of the bushwhackers. What should I do now? I realized that I couldn't go on to Jem because there'd be lots more Yankee cavalry along the way. Yet I couldn't start out for Georgia without him.

If I was ever to get to my brother through miles and miles of strange country held by Yankees, I'd need the help of somebody older and wiser than I was. And that would be just one person in the world—Rosellen Sanders. She had helped us in Roswell. I'd go to her in Cannelton over the Ohio River in Indiana. Then together we'd come to Hartford and get Jem.

Knowing what I had to do now, I got up and began to walk again. I retraced my steps and finally got to the crossroads. I sat there the rest of that night and waited for somebody to come along and give me directions. Toward morning a family traveling in a wagon showed me the road that went north to the Ohio River and Indiana. I thanked them kindly and bought some food from them. They were good folks and wished me Godspeed as I went on my way.

Other folks with wagons passed me by, but nobody

asked me to ride with them. By sundown that day, my feet were so hot and swelled up I was glad to cool them in a roadside creek. That night I slept in an old deserted cabin. The ladder to the loft was strong enough to hold me, so I climbed up and hauled the ladder in after me. That way nobody and nothing could get to me.

A day and a half of walking brought me to Hawesville and the Ohio River. The town was just one long street on top of a levee over the water. I went right down to the Ohio and stood on a dock, looking across to Indiana.

As I stared at the river, wondering how to cross it, a round-as-a-barrel woman in a tan shawl and brown bonnet came up to stand beside me. She asked, "Are you waiting for the ferry, too, my lad?"

"Ferry, ma'am?"

"Why, of course—it should be coming along soon." She gave me a strange look and pointed to a wooden sign a few feet from me. "This is where the Indiana ferryboat docks. She's due in fifteen minutes' time."

I asked, "What does it cost to ride on the ferry?" I figured it probably wouldn't be free.

"Five cents." She looked at me strangely again and added, "It says five cents on the sign. Can't you read, son?"

"No, ma'am, not too well—not yet. I know the ABC's and I can put 'em together to make some words, but not a lot of 'em yet."

She sighed. "Oh my! There are so many young ones here who cannot read and write, let alone figure. Are you going to Cannelton? Do you have friends there?"

I was careful how I replied and told her slowly, "Yes, my brother's wife is workin' in a cloth mill there. I come up here from Hartford where my other brother and me were workin' on a farm."

"Then you're just visiting her?"

"No, ma'am. It's my hope to be taken on in the mill where she works. I can earn more workin' in a mill than I can on a farm, and my family sure can use the extra money."

"My, but you do have a lot of family feeling," the lady said.

"I truly do. My whole family does. We all like to stick together all of the time."

"Commendable, most commendable. It was most pleasant talking with you, my lad. I hope you will find everything goes well for you in Cannelton."

I asked, "Do you know anybody in the mills there?"

"Gracious, yes. I know the owners, Mr. Joseph and Mr. Francis Greenwood. Everybody knows them. They're the most important men in town and very fine gentlemen, too."

The lady soon left me to talk to another woman a distance away. I was glad to be left alone. I stood, my hands in my pockets, looking at the blue river and pondering. How would Rosellen take to seeing me dressed up in boy's duds and hearing that I had run away from the Fletchers? It had been a month and more since I'd seen her, and I had lots to tell her.

I crossed the Ohio on a stern-wheeler steamboat. I stood at the end of the steamer to watch the wheel churn up the river. It was the first boat ride I had ever had, and I liked it. The ride to Louisville had been my first train ride, but I certainly hadn't enjoyed that journey. The crossing didn't take long, and soon the boat stopped at a dock on the other side of the Ohio. I walked down a plank and stepped out onto Indiana.

There was a wagon and a team of horses waiting for the woman who had talked to me at the ferry crossing, but she didn't offer me a ride. I didn't need one anyway. Cannelton was right on the river. It wasn't a big town, but it was neat and tidy. It was filled with wood houses and shops, and wagons and buggies went up and down the streets. The folks walked fast, like they were on their way to something important. Louisville people had walked fast, too, come to think about it. Maybe it was the Northern way of walking.

Because I was a mill hand by trade, I recognized the Cannelton mill right off. It was a truly big building made of gray stone. It had four stories and two tall, sharp-pointed towers in the middle. As I came near, I recognized the banging and thumping sounds coming from it. They were the same kinds of noises I remembered from home.

While I stood looking and listening, my innards were telling me it was nigh on to suppertime. Though I hadn't eaten good since I left Louisville, my insides hadn't forgotten what it was like to eat at the right time. I was hoping that Rosellen would be coming out soon to eat supper. I reckoned that the work hours here would be pretty much the same as they had been in Roswell. So I sat down on the grass and faced the big front doors of the mill, figuring this to be where the mill hands would be coming out.

I was right. The bell in one of the steeples rang shortly after I sat down, and a minute or so later, workers came streaming out. I got up and started forward, looking at each face as the mill hands hurried past me. I *had* to find Rosellen. I was running out of money. I was weary, and my feet were sore. I was tired of keeping up my grit and of being alone. I needed her.

She was among the last of the lot to come out. She shone with cleanliness in a bright blue muslin dress with a white collar and cuffs and a long white apron. Her gold hair was tied back with a blue ribbon bow, and she wore a snood. She started out of the big doors, then stopped just outside and looked back as if she'd been called to. I saw a tall young man walk up to her and bend his head to talk. I recognized him as the young man with deep red hair who had hired her in Louisville. Rosellen looked up at him and frowned. Then I saw her nod and look away. She nodded again and started walking directly toward me, leaving him staring hard after her.

She would have gone right past me if I hadn't run up to her to say, "Rosellen, it's me, *Hannalee*. I ain't a boy. I run away from Louisville."

She stopped in her tracks and whirled to stare at me. Then she grabbed hold of me and hugged me to her. When she let me go, I saw tears in her eyes. She said softly so the other mill girls passing us couldn't hear, "Hannalee, are you all right? Why're you dressed like a boy?"

"I had to, to get here. I'm all right, but I'm hungry."

"Come along with me. I'm goin' to my boardin'house for supper."

"Can I go there, too?"

"Yes, I'll tell Miz Burton about you. She'll feed you tonight." As we went along close together, how happy I was just to be with her.

I told her about Jem being taken away by the farmer, and how I couldn't get to him so decided to come to her instead. I also told her about old Miz Fletcher and why I had to run away from Louisville. When I finished, I asked her, "How you been? You look fine, Rosellen."

She was biting her lower lip now as she said, "I can't complain. It's not half so bad here as I thought it'd be, even if it is a Yankee mill. The pay's better, and we Southern mill hands ain't treated bad. I ain't heard 'Secesh' once. Mr. Joseph and Mr. Francis Greenwood won't allow that."

"Was that Mr. Greenwood I saw you talkin' with just now?"

She gave me a flashing glance. "Yes, that was Mr. Francis. He's the son. He and his father are good men, even if they are Yankees. Mr. Francis suffers from a sickness called asthma. That's why he's not in the Union Army."

I wasn't one bit interested in him. Instead I wanted to know, "Will you run away with me tonight so we can get Jem and all go home together?"

Rosellen stopped in her tracks. She swung me around to face her and said, "No, I won't run away with you tonight! And let me tell you why. You saw Mr. Francis call me back just now. Well, he had bad news to tell me. He found out over the telegraph this afternoon that Atlanta fell to the Yankees. Our Gen'ral Johnston, the one your brother Davey liked so much, was kicked out weeks ago, and a Gen'ral Hood took over for him. There was fightin' around Atlanta earlier, but Hood decided to quit defendin' the city. So he marched our soldiers out of Atlanta to God knows where, and the Yankees have marched in."

"Atlanta *can't* be Yankee now!"

"Well, it is. That means that all of north Georgia is probably in Yankee hands. So are Tennessee and Kentucky." Rosellen shook me a little by the shoulders. "Oh, Hannalee, I made up my mind the first week here that I wouldn't try to get back to Roswell till the war ended. Mr. Francis thinks it won't be long now before that happens. Hannalee, the South is losin' to the North. It's bein' beat to its knees. It hasn't got enough money or men or enough friends to go on much longer. You know how poor we lived in Roswell—on corn bread and sowbelly. That's how our army lives, too, and it tries to fight hard and to win, though it's hungry. Sometimes when I was in Roswell workin', I thought I'd drop from pure weariness and hunger. I can work twice as fast and twice as hard here in this mill."

I drew myself away from Rosellen and looked at her. How pink her cheeks were and how bright her eyes. The good Yankee victuals had done that, made her prettier and stronger than ever. I told her, "I bet Davey ain't eatin' so good as you."

This made her mad. She told me, "I just told you that. But your brother wouldn't begrudge any one of us good food and a good bed to sleep in. He'd want us to have that, Hannalee. He'd understand why I work here for the Yankees rather than go to one of their jailhouses." Suddenly she asked, "Do the folks you worked for in Louisville know where you might be headed?"

"I don't know, truly. The man there knows I had kin in Hartford and that I knew somebody in Cannelton."

Rosellen looked me up and down. Then she muttered, "If there were wanted notices, they'd be about a hired girl named Hannalee Reed. There might even be a reward for gettin' hold of you. But now that you're dressed like a boy, you could be all right here in Cannelton. You'd best stay a boy, and we'll just keep cuttin' your hair short whenever it starts gettin' long. But I think the name of Reed ought to go. If there *is* a notice and you're named Reed in it, it could fetch you trouble. What did you call yourself as a boy?"

"Hannibal."

"Hannibal?" Rosellen made a face, then said, "All right, be that, then. I go by Rosellen Reed here, the name I gave the Yankees down in Louisville. You be Hannibal Sanders. Use my real last name."

As we went up the steps of a neat, two-story stone house together, Rosellen stopped and told me, "This is Miz Burton's house. I'll tell her you're Hannibal Sanders, Kentucky kin of my ma's folks. There's no call to let her know you're a Roswell mill hand, too, or a runaway from Louisville. I'll tell her you worked in a mill in Kentucky as a bobbin boy, and that when our folks told you where I'm workin' now, you come here to see if I could get you a job in the Cannelton mill. She'll have room for you because a girl mill hand just left this morning to go to work in Indianapolis. But you'll be expected to do some boy chores for her. Her husband and sons are in the Yankee army, so there's no men hereabouts. I'll get you work in our mill as a bobbin boy. They need new hands."

Now Rosellen opened the dark green door and we went inside a long, narrow hallway that smelled good of roasting meat and polished furniture. It wasn't until I was halfway down the hallway that it came to me that Rosellen had called herself *Rosellen* Reed, not *Mrs. Davey* Reed.

I caught hold of her and whispered, "Are you Mrs. Davey Reed here?"

"No, I'm not. Miz Burton knows I'm not married."

A cold feeling came over me. I could see that Rosellen had changed up here in Yankee land. It wasn't just her new clothes. She was different in ways I couldn't put my finger on. I slid my hand into my pants pocket to take hold of Mama's persimmon-seed button. As always, the feel of it gave me comfort. It didn't change!

Chapter Seven

More Months

Miz Burton had eyes as blue as the noontime skies at home and soft white hair that fell down in ringlets around her face. She was dressed rich, in plum-colored taffeta with a white lace collar and purple brooch. Right off, she was friendly and welcomed me.

She told me, "I'm Mrs. Charlotte Burton, Hannibal. My husband and sons are serving in the Union Army in Virginia. Do you have family in the army, too?"

I looked at Rosellen, wondering what to say, but she didn't speak out or give me any signs to help me out. I decided to tell the Yankee lady the truth. "Ma'am, I got two brothers. Both of 'em used to be mill workers like me. One of 'em's workin' now for a farmer near Hartford, Kentucky. You may not like hearin' about the other one, though, and may turn me out for it. My other brother's in the Confederate Army in Virginia."

Her face didn't change. She said, "Yes, I suppose your family would be Confederate, wouldn't it? I know Rosellen's sad tale. She has told me how the soldiers took her away to Louisville. I think that was a most wicked thing for the army to do to poor mill hands. Rosellen wasn't a soldier. Burning the mill in her town should have been enough to suit General Sherman. He must be a most severe sort of person."

I didn't say a word. I surely hadn't expected any Yankee to talk like that, to agree with what I was thinking.

Miz Burton went on, "Rosellen isn't the only mill hand from the South with me now. There's little Sally Fox, who worked as a bobbin girl in New Manchester, Georgia. She is thirteen. That's rather near your age, Hannibal, isn't it? Where did you work in Kentucky?"

Rosellen answered for me. "Near to Munfordville. Hannibal said he left it 'cause it was a firetrap. He's an orphan, you know."

"Are you, Hannibal? I'm sorry to hear that. What did you do in your mill?"

"He was a bobbin boy," Rosellen said fast.

I'd almost said bobbin *girl*. I could see that it wasn't going to be so easy to be Hannibal on the outside when on the inside I was Hannalee, but I had to do it.

"A bobbin boy?" Miz Charlotte smiled and nodded. "I know mill work, too. One of my sons used to be a bobbin boy in the Greenwoods' mill. I am sure they can use your services." To my surprise, she put her arm around my shoulders. I liked her doing that. I didn't shy off when she said, "I've needed a boy around the place to chop wood and fill the kitchen woodbox. I miss my lads. Tell me, Hannibal, do you read and write?"

"A little bit—I know the ABC's and some words."

"Would you like to learn more while you're here? I was once a schoolteacher, and I'm teaching Sally Fox every evening after work."

I couldn't believe my ears! To live in a house with a real live teacher. "Oh, ma'am, I'd like that. I truly would."

"Good. Now, wouldn't you like a cup of milk? You look a bit peaked."

"Thank you, I surely would."

When she left to go to her pantry, Rosellen told me, "You did just fine. This is the best boardin' house in Cannelton. Other Yankees here ain't so kindly natured as Miz Burton. I work hard at the mill. I mind my own business, and I don't talk much about the war. I listen and bear in mind all the time that this is Yankee land. Nobody here knows anythin' much about me, and I'd be obliged if you didn't tell anybody about how we were in Georgia."

"You didn't ever tell anybody about Davey or Jem or me or your Aunt Marilla?"

"No, it wasn't anythin' that concerns the folks here."

"All right, I won't say a word about anythin'." I'd keep hushed up even though I couldn't say I liked what she had just told me.

After I finished the milk she brought me, Miz Burton

showed me to a little room at the back of the house that had a bed, a chair, a chest of drawers, and a washstand with a jug and basin on it. There was a hand-stitched red and yellow quilt on the bed. It was a fine room, and she had a fine house, and I hoped she'd serve up a supper to match.

She surely did—pork chops and gravy. Sitting at the table, I met her other boarders. The other Georgia girl, Sally Fox, was sandy-headed and freckly, and she barely peeped at me while she ate. Besides Sally, there were two Indiana mill girls who worked as spinners. One was tall, thin, and sharp-nosed, with a floury face and vinegary ways; and the other was a brown-headed butterball of a girl. Though they were as different as daylight and darkness, they were both named Elizabeth. The tall one was called Lizzie and the fat one Betty. Because they were older than me and also had more important jobs at the mill, they didn't pay me much heed.

For all her kind ways, Miz Burton saw to it that things ran smooth in her house and that the house rules were kept. I learned that right away. After they finished eating, the mill hands ran back to work, and I went out to the woodpile to start my work, too. I was sure glad I'd sometimes chopped wood at home for Mama, so I knew how to do it. When I finished filling her woodbox, Miz Charlotte told me what she expected of her boarders. She said that they couldn't ever chew tobacco or rest their elbows on the table or drink out of saucers. She also told me how proud she was of Rosellen's improvement in manners, that she was becoming a regular lady, and that there was no reason why a mill worker couldn't have the manners of a lady or of a gentleman.

I thought about this. Rosellen certainly had changed, and Miz Burton was helping her. Rosellen always had fine and fancy ways, and now she was getting daintier. Looking at her across the table, I'd been reminded of some china statues I used to dust on Miz Fletcher's mantel. They were pink and white and gold, and as pretty as could be. No matter how hot the day had been, they were always cool to a person's touch. Rosellen was like one of them now.

After the mill hands came home that night, Miz Burton sat Sally Fox and me down at her parlor table and gave us slates, chalk, and books. My heart beat so fast I thought it would jump out of me. She put us through our ABC's and made us do some figuring. Then she leaned back in her chair and said, "Well, Hannibal, I'd say you and Sally do about the same, wouldn't you? Sally couldn't even recite the alphabet when she first came here. You've both worked hard tonight."

Hearing such warm words gave me the courage to ask Miz Burton something that had come into my head. Touching Mama's button in my pocket, I asked, "Miz Burton, do you think you could help Sally or Rosellen write a letter home to Georgia to let their folks know they're all right?" Truly, it was me who wanted to write the letter home, but I couldn't say that, since I was supposed to be from Kentucky.

My idea didn't set well with Miz Burton. She stared at me in amazement and said, "Why, certainly not, Hannibal. Such a thing is impossible. You cannot write a letter to someone in a country that is at war with your country and expect it to be delivered. A person would be crazy to try. What a thing to suggest! But then, of course, you're only a child and couldn't know. Oh, how cruel and hard this war is! I wish there was some way, Sally, to let your family know about you, but there simply is not. Pray that the war will soon be over. They say it can't last much longer now that Atlanta has fallen."

Sally asked softly, "The Confederacy's losin', huh?"

"It appears that way."

I said, "The war ain't over yet!"

Miz Burton patted my head. "No, Hannibal, it isn't. Now, let's try some more arithmetic and reading. I want to start the two of you on a reader as quickly as I can. When you go home, Sally, I want you to go reading and writing. As for you, Hannibal, perhaps you'd like me to help you write your brother in Hartford someday soon?"

Write Jem? Yes, I'd like to do that just fine, but I'd rather write to Mama.

The next morning I went to the mill with Rosellen and Sally. With Rosellen speaking up for me, I was hired on as a bobbin boy right away. Once again I sat with a bobbin box at my feet and schoolwork in my hands. The mill noises were loud as ever, and the signals the weavers gave me when they wanted bobbins were the same as in Roswell's mill. But here they were making blue uniform cloth, not gray.

And so I started to work in the Cannelton mill, going back and forth to it every day but Sunday, just as I'd gone to our own mill before.

The mill became familiar to me soon, probably because it was so similar to the one in Georgia. Its big wheel worked the same, with the water pouring over it, turning it and the long axle that went into the mill where more wheels turned to power the looms. The wooden looms flew back and forth, *click-boom, click-boom*. Bobbins full of thread spun on the spinning floor sat atop the looms, and the thread was fed down into the looms, making cloth. I never tired of watching the big looms work and seeing the girls tie weavers' knots to keep a piece of weaving going. If it wasn't for the blue-dyed cloth in the looms, I could tell myself I was back home, not in Indiana at all.

Even though I pined for home, I could tell that Rosellen didn't. She was drawing further and further away from me all the time. I could feel it when we walked together to and from the mill during the day. She walked faster and faster, not saying much, and kept her head turned away from me. She usually didn't look at me or the other girls at meals, either. What was the matter with her, I asked myself?

One day toward the end of September, when we were coming home at the end of the day, I finally decided to ask her. "You don't seem to be the same as you used to be in Roswell."

Her eyes narrowed as she turned her head to stare at me. She told me, "I'm not! You're not either, Hannalee."

"Yes, I am."

She shook her head. "No, you ain't the same, and it ain't just that you wear boy's clothes. You're diff'runt. Jem'll be diff'runt, too. We've all had a lot of things happen to us since last July. If we do go home, we won't be goin' back to Roswell the same folks we was when we were taken away. It'd be easier if we could write letters to our family and get letters back." Rosellen sighed. "But let me tell you, Hannalee Reed, I wouldn't have writ to your brother Davey if I could have! He probably cares even less for me now than he did in July."

I flared at her. "You're his true love, Rosellen. Does it still stick in your craw that he wouldn't marry you when you asked him to?"

Her voice was so soft I could hardly hear it. "I shouldn't have asked him to make me his wife then. His sayin' no to me cost me dearly in my pride. I know pride's a sin, and I got too much of it, but that's how I am by nature."

Speaking quietly, too, though there was nobody near enough to hear us, I told her, "He wouldn't marry you because he didn't want to leave you his widow. He's proud, too."

Her face crumpled, and her eyes filled with tears. "Hannalee, I'd rather be his grievin' widow and have had one day of bein' his lovin' wife than have nothin' at all the way I do now."

"Rosellen, he loves you dearly. He'll go out of his mind when he hears the Yankees took us all the way to Indiana."

Now she almost yelled at me. "What good'll that do us? Davey won't ever be comin' up here with the Confederate Army. His army is stayin' put where it is in Virginia. If any Confederate soldiers do come up through Kentucky, it won't be him." Rosellen looked hatchets at me now. "The South is losin' the war! Anybody with any horse sense knows it. Our soldiers have fought hard for three years now. They're worn out. You saw the Southern cavalry that come to burn our bridge in Roswell. You saw that they were gray in the face. You saw how skinny Davey was and how he coughed. Do you think our other soldiers look better? Look at me. *Look at you.* We eat good Yankee food, not just corn bread and sowbelly like we did back home. I know our folks are hungry, and it aches me, but I go on eatin' all the same. Don't you ever speak your brother's name to me again! I'll love Davey

Reed all the days of my life and hold him in my heart, but don't you say his name to me again! He said no twice when it came to marryin'. Hannalee, you leave me alone about him. Leave me be now!"

She cried out silently like a wild bird would and clapped her hands over her ears as if to shut out what I might say. Then she ran from me, her cloak flapping out around her.

I didn't run after her. What she'd told me made me feel more lonesome than ever. The North was gray and cold for me. It took blood kin around a person to keep out homesickness, and Rosellen wasn't, even less now than ever before. Her heart had changed toward me and my kin. She'd never again hear the name of Davey Reed from me.

Later that week I asked Miz Burton to help me write a letter to Jem. I hoped he'd find somebody there to read it to him and then answer me. I told him where I was and that I was working in a mill and living in the same house as Rosellen. I wrote that I hoped he was bearing up well and would not forget his relation. Then I signed it "Hann. Sanders." I knew Jem would figure out why I was "Hann. Sanders."

Each day after that, I looked for a letter from him, but October passed and nothing ever came. I fretted over not hearing. Where was Jem? What had happened to him? Had he run away from the farmer the way I had from the Fletchers? I longed for home and Mama. I thought about her and Jem and Davey day and night, wondering how they were. It galled me to be here in Indiana, waiting for Rosellen to tell me she'd go with me to look for Jem and then head home to Georgia.

But even though I kept hoping Rosellen would finally decide it was time to leave, I didn't see any signs of that happening. For one thing, she didn't save her pay for the trip back home like me and Sally Fox did.

I wasn't the only person who noticed this, either. The other mill girls who boarded with Miz Burton did, too. One night after work, while Rosellen was up in her room and Miz Charlotte was still in the kitchen, I was sitting with Sally and the two Elizabeths in the parlor. We were talking about the mill when Lizzie said spitefully, "Well, I'm sure we all know why that sly puss Rosellen Reed primps all the time now, fussing over her appearance. The next thing we know, she'll take up drinking chalk and vinegar to make her cheeks pale."

I asked, "Why would she do that?"

Betty giggled. "She's making herself prettier for somebody at the mill, that's why."

I asked Betty, "Who?"

"Mr. Francis Greenwood, that's who. Everybody on that floor of the mill's talking about him and her. They say she's caught his eye and he's been comin' in and out of the mill drawin' room a lot more often now than he ever used to."

Lizzie went on, full of spite and envy. "He and Rosellen have a lot to say to one another these days."

I told her, "Mr. Francis tells her about how the war's goin' on."

Betty laughed. "Oh, fumadiddle! Is that what you think, Hannibal? Womenfolks notice things like this. You boys don't. You never see what's at the end of your noses. Besides, you don't get down to Rosellen's floor to see what goes on in there. Sometimes Mr. Francis stands very close to her stool to watch her work. He bends *right over* her!"

I said, "He's just showin' her the pattern he wants her to make in the cloth, that's all."

"Is it? I think he's smitten with Rosellen." Lizzie turned harder. "What difference does it make to you, Hannibal? She's not that close a kin for you to care if a Union man is interested in her."

I got up. "It don't make any diff'runce to me. It's her bus'ness and his bus'ness, and it ain't yours, either." I tromped out and went up to my room to get my reader for my lessons with Miz Burton. Though I was plenty angry, I wouldn't let on to anybody that I was, and I sure didn't want to hear talk about Rosellen and Mr. Francis Greenwood.

November brought bad news for us Southerners by telegraph in the middle of the month. That cussed old General Sherman, who had taken us mill hands away, had marched out of Atlanta with sixty thousand soldiers, burning down everything there first so our own army wouldn't find anything to help them if they ever got that city back again. From Atlanta, Sherman planned to go all the way to the sea at Savannah.

Just thinking about what he was up to made me feel sick to my stomach. What if he went through Roswell on his way? Would he shoot people? What would happen to Mama and the baby that must be born by now, if the Yankees came again?

I couldn't share my fears for the South with anybody, and especially not with Rosellen. By now I knew that what Lizzie and Betty had said was true. Mr. Francis was mightily interested in her. I'd seen him walk out of the mill with her, and once I saw him take her arm to steer her clear of a puddle in her path. She looked up at him and smiled, then looked away blushing when he went on staring at her. And one Sunday he came to Miz Burton's house and had tea with her and Rosellen in the parlor. Then Rosellen had put on her bonnet and pelisse and had gone out riding with him. She'd walked out right past me, not looking me in the face. Davey had lost her! In the bottom of my heart I knew it. Even if she did still love him, the fact that she went out with Mr. Francis meant that she didn't expect ever to be Mrs. Davey Reed. She'd never go away home with me now.

I grieved for Davey and his lost love. And I finally

made up my mind. I couldn't stay here anymore. I couldn't work in the mill and see her with Mr. Francis and hear what folks were saying about them. I couldn't stay here worrying about Mama and the baby now that General Sherman was fighting in Georgia. I couldn't go on wondering why Jem had never answered my letter.

I had to find out how my folks were for myself.

The morning after I heard about General Sherman being in Georgia again, I got up out of bed long before I had to go to the mill. By lantern light I took the sheets off my bed and piled them on top of it to be washed. I put a dollar on the pillow to pay Miz Charlotte what I owed to her. Then I put the nine dollars I had left into my pants pocket next to Mama's persimmon-seed button, put on the winter jacket, scarf, and cap I'd bought, and left as quiet as could be by the back door. Although I could write a note now, I didn't leave one. There was just too much I would want to say. I'd have told Miz Burton that I never would have believed before I knew her that I could like a Yankee. I'd learned by now that there were good and bad Yankees, as well as good and bad Confederates. As for Rosellen, I would have thanked her for what she'd done for Jem and me when we left Roswell, but she already knew I was grateful to her. She'd know, too, how I felt about her and Mr. Francis. She hadn't looked me straight in the face since she'd gone out in the buggy with him, and I'd stopped walking to the mill with her. She knew that I would leave her be. And I knew she'd let me go in peace, too. Rosellen'd know why I went and probably where I was going, but she wouldn't tell anybody.

I kissed Miz Burton's school book and slate and left them on my bed. As a token of her, I kept the pencil she gave me. She'd notice that and maybe remember me and not think I was a thief because I took it.

As the sun rose, I was at the dock waiting for the first ferry of the day to cross the Ohio to Hawesville. When I got aboard, I went up to the bow so as not to look back at Indiana. Instead, I looked up at the flocks of birds flying overhead. The wild geese had already flown by. I'd heard them weeks ago during the night, and had gone outside to look for them. They were going south where I wanted to go. My heart had cried out to fly away then, too. Now I was finally going home.

Chapter Eight

The Last Day
of November

I WASN'T SO SCARED NOW AS I'D BEEN WHEN I STARTED away from the Fletcher house in Louisville. I knew the country here because I'd walked over it. I went through Hawesville and back along the road I'd walked last August, but now I shivered where I'd roasted then.

Hardly anybody was on the road, and it rained almost all the way to Hartford—two days of rain. I spent only a dollar of my money for food, and I didn't spend a cent on a place to sleep. A couple of barns did just dandy for me. One time I slept in a hayloft under a borrowed horse blanket, and the other time in a clean, empty stall next door to a black-and-white cow. When the roosters crowed, I'd get up and get out and away before anybody even saw me.

I went fast as I could, recalling Quantrill and the Yankee horse soldiers, but I never saw more than two men riding along in the rain or a few folks in wagons and buggies.

I arrived in Hartford in late afternoon. It was a little

town, and only one place there held any interest for me
—the post office. In Cannelton, Miz Burton had told me
that post office folks knew where people lived. So I
headed for it to ask the whereabouts of a farmer by the
name of Rufus Hopkins. The post office had to know!

A big, redheaded lady told me that Mr. Hopkins was
some two to three miles out of town to the west. She went
to the door of the post office with me, pointed to the road
I was to take, and said, "You'll know his place by the sign
on the gate. It says: 'Hopkins—hogs, eggs, and corn.' Can
you read, son?"

"Yes, ma'am, I can read some." I knew most of those
words, and I reckoned "Hopkins" had some of the same
letters to start with as "hogs." I thanked her kindly and
went on my way.

It wasn't long before I was at the split-rail fence with
the white sign on it painted in black letters. By now it
was raining harder and blowing some, too, so I was
bone-cold. There wasn't anybody in sight, and in the big,
whitewashed house made of logs there wasn't a lamp in
any window, though it was getting on to dusk. As I
looked at the Hopkins farm, I wondered if Jem was still
here, or if he'd run off home a long time back. Could that
be why he didn't answer to my letter?

I went under the fence, walked along a line of trees that
appeared to be a young orchard, and got to the rear of
the house. There I saw the barn, a hogpen, and a chipyard

with a log pile. There was also a good-sized building to store grain, and a big chicken coop. I went to the barn door and opened it, then slid inside. Tobacco hung from the rafters above me. I climbed up the ladder to the hayloft and flopped down in front of a big crack in the hayloft wall. That crack gave me a fine view of the back of the Hopkins house. A gray-and-white barn cat came over and lay down beside me after a while.

As I watched from my hiding place, a tall, tow-headed girl and a smaller one came inside the barn to tend to the two mules, the cows, and the old horse beneath me. After they left, the lamps were lit in the house and went out later. The cat and I kept each other company all night long as I lay in the loft shivering and wondering about my brother Jem.

The first call of the rooster woke me up from a little sleep the next morning, and I came down the ladder, carrying the cat with me. I knew somebody would come out of the house to gather the eggs laid during the night. I'd prayed it would be Jem. A stout, yellow-haired woman came out and stood on the back steps flapping dust out of a rug. When she finished, she went right inside again.

Then the door opened once more, and I wanted to shout with joy. Jem came out. He looked fine. He was a mite taller than I recalled him, but it was Jem coming toward the hen house with an egg basket in one hand. I set the cat down and followed him into the hen coop full of white laying hens on roosts. As Jem reached under the first hen and came out with an egg in his hand, I said softly, "Jemmie Reed, it's me, your sister, Hannalee. I come to fetch you away."

He jerked around and dropped the egg, letting it bust on the floor. He stared and stared at me while the chickens clucked and fluttered. Then he cried softly, "It *is* you, *you* dressed like a boy. Where'd you come from, Hannalee?"

"Indiana, Jem. Didn't you get the letter I sent you?"

"No, I never got no letter from anybody."

"Well, I sent you one. Mebbe your old farmer kept it. Come on. You got on a jacket and a cap, so you don't need to go back to the house. Can we get away from here without our bein' seen?"

"Oh, Hannalee!" Suddenly Jem put down the egg basket, grabbed hold of me, and gave me a hug. He said, "It'll be easy to leave. You come at the right time. Hopkins and his other girl went to Hartford yesterday in the rig and stayed overnight at his old ma's house. They won't be back till later on today. We can go behind the barn to another road. If Hopkins is on his way back, he'll be on a diff'runt one. I *knowed* you'd come for me. Hannalee, where're we goin'?"

"There ain't but one place to go. Home!"

"That's where I want to go more'n anywheres in the

world." He drew back. "But I ain't got any money at all."

"I have. I been workin' in a Yankee mill. Come along, now. What about the womenfolks in the house?"

"They're fixin' breakfast. They won't come out here for a while."

"Good. Let's go, Jem."

We went out behind the barn fast, ducked under a fence, and crossed a pasture. Then we went under another fence and were on the road Jem knew. He said that it went west to Missouri and northeast to Louisville.

I nodded. "Louisville's where we want to go. We can get us a train there."

As we walked together, I took his hand. How good and strong my brother's hand felt. We walked along in silence for a while. Then Jem asked me, "Won't the Yankee soldiers in Louisville be after us?"

"Mebbe so, mebbe not. They'll be huntin' for a girl, anyhow, not two boys. Jem, I want to get us on a train for Georgia. When I was in Indiana, I got news that the same bluebelly gen'ral who dragged us away from Roswell is travelin' in Georgia again. I think we ought to go home now no matter what. Mama may need us bad."

"Hannalee, the baby ought to be here by now, huh?"

"That's right. Baby Paul's born now."

As we sat down to rest under some trees after walking a few miles, I told Jem about the Fletchers and meeting up with Quantrill. He listened and then told me, "I bet old Miz Fletcher looked like the hind wheels of bad luck. You had a bad time, Hannalee. I had it better with old Hopkins, though he didn't take to me, either. He didn't whip me or call me a mawmouth or a Secesh. But he worked me hard and didn't ever pay me. I curried his stock and milked the cows and weeded the corn and tobacco and did everythin' else he told me to do. Now that it's wintertime, he don't need a hired hand much. He won't send after me. He always said I et too much for my keep and the work I did. Tell me about Rosellen. Have you seen her?"

"Jem, I been livin' in the same house with her some months and workin' in the same mill she works in. That's where I went when I couldn't get here to you the first time I tried." I sighed. "Jemmie, Rosellen ain't the same. She loves Davey, but I think she's givin' up on him. She didn't allow me to say his name to her. She's prettier'n she ever was on the outside, but inside she's changed her heart. She didn't want to leave with me when I asked her to the first day I came to Indiana. I didn't even trouble myself to ask her along when I left a couple days ago. She's doin' real fine in the Yankee mill, better'n she did in Georgia."

I decided not to tell him about Mr. Francis Greenwood. It didn't make good telling and would make poor hearing. I said, "I went on with my schoolin' with a decent-natured Yankee lady. There are some of 'em.

When we get home to Mama, I plan to write a letter to Davey."

"What'll you say to him about Rosellen?"

I didn't answer. I only looked at Jem. He had worry in his eyes. Water was running off the brim of his cap, and I saw that he didn't have anything to keep his neck warm. I unwound my scarf, put it around his neck, and tied it. Then I turned up my collar to keep me warm.

He grinned and said, "Thank you, Hannalee."

"No, not Hannalee—*Hannibal!* Don't forget that name. And when we get to Louisville, don't you forget to do what I tell you to."

"You sound a lot like Rosellen did on our way up here."

"Mebbe so. Mebbe I learned somethin' from her. Now let's get up and get on the way again. Do you know someplace dry where we can sleep tonight where nobody'll find us?"

"Sure I do. It come to me to run off, too, but I didn't know where to find you or Rosellen, and I didn't want to go all by my lonesome. Whenever I went someplace with Hopkins, I kept my eyes open for hidin' places just in case I ever got my gumption up high enough to go."

"Oh, Jemmie!" I flung my arm around his shoulder and for a second held him close to me. "I'm glad you stayed. I'm so glad you were still here when I come for you. Jem, I want to show you somethin' I been keepin' secret."

I reached into my pants pocket and brought out the persimmon-seed button. Jem knew it by sight. He cried, "It's Mama's!"

"Yes, I'm takin' it home to her. She gave it to me and told me to fetch it back to her. But I'm bringin' her more'n that. I'm fetchin' you, too. We'll both take it back to her."

Getting ourselves to Louisville was hard, since we had to walk all the way; and it took quite a while because we got so sore-footed, and Jem wasn't so long-legged as I was. I was surely weary of putting one foot in front of the other by the time we got there.

Once we found the railroad depot, I'd planned to buy two tickets to the very end of Tennessee, so all we'd have to do was walk over the border into Georgia. But it didn't turn out that way. When Jem and I went up to the ticket window and I asked how far south we could go in the state of Tennessee, the ticket seller told me, "That'll be Nashville, lad. We don't go any farther south. If you want to get farther down the line, you'll have to get on another railroad in Nashville."

Nashville? Yes, that's where we'd been put on another train back in July. I reckoned that getting there would get us halfway home.

"How much will two tickets to Nashville cost me?"

"How old are you, son? And how old's the boy with you?"

"I'm twelve. He's ten."

"That'll be two half fares, then."

It cost plenty of money, but I paid him in Yankee metal coins, my Cannelton wages. He gave me two paper tickets, saying, "You board at four o'clock. The train's number 33. Will you be able to find it? Can you read?"

"Yes, sir, I can find it. I know my numbers."

I gave Jem his ticket, then we went away to buy things to eat on the way to Nashville. We had two hours before the train left, but after we bought some popovers at a bakery near the depot, we just sat on a bench in the train station and waited. I was afraid that if we wandered around Louisville, Miz Fletcher might spot me, even though I was dressed as a boy. If she caught hold of me, I was sure she'd try to put me in a Yankee jailhouse. Close to four o'clock we got on the train, and once it left the depot, I breathed easy again.

It was truly different going back to Nashville than coming up. We weren't prisoners now, and we were sitting on cushioned seats, not wood benches. And this time we were going home—not leaving. Each time the railroad car wheels went a-clickity, we got closer.

After three days our train finally pulled into Nashville, on the twenty-ninth of the month, into the very same station we'd been before. It looked just the same, crawling with Yankee soldiers. This time, though, they looked grim-faced and sour.

I told Jem softly, "Look at 'em. Somethin's botherin' 'em. It's got to be somethin' about the war. Let's go find out what it is."

Jem asked, "Could you mebbe read a newspaper?"

"That won't be easy, but I'll try."

We went over to a boy who had a pile of papers at his feet, and I gave him a penny for one of them. As he handed me the paper, I asked, "What does it say about Gen'ral Sherman, who's supposed to be goin' down through Georgia now?"

"Nothin'. Old Cump Sherman started out earlier this month, but he don't send any news back. Nobody knows what's happenin' in Georgia. It's General Hood who's makin' the news right here in Tennessee."

"Why's that?"

The boy laughed at me. "Where you been, kid? General Hood's come up here, and he's got a whole Confederate army here right now. I hear tell he's camped just a hoot and holler away from us here in Nashville. He's just down the road at Franklin. There'll be a fight soon, and it'll be a big one!"

Our army so near? I turned my face away so the newsboy wouldn't see how excited I was at that news. Jem and I walked out of the depot, threading our way in and out of Yankee soldiers. We sat down on a curbing and I looked at the paper, trying to read it. I saw the name "Hood" and the word "Franklin" over and over.

While I tried to make sense out of the big words in the paper, I was also pondering the news. I told Jem slowly, "When it gets dark, you and I are headin' for Franklin. It's got to be south of here somewheres. We'll find our own soldiers and tell 'em who we are. They'll let us through their lines so we can go on home. Once they whip the Yankees up here, all the rest of the state of Tennessee ought to be Confederate, so it'll be easy goin' for us. All we got to do is keep travelin' south. If there are any Yankees still around, I reckon Gen'ral Hood'll march down and clear 'em out once he wins up here in Tennessee."

Jem asked, "What if there are bluebellies in Roswell?"

"Why should there be any with the mill burned and the mill hands gone away? There could be, though. Some could'a been left there."

Jem looked sad. "Do you reckon most of the mill hands'll come home soon, too?"

"I dunno. I know two who are goin' to, though, and that's what interests me right now. It'll be dark soon. By then we got to find the road that goes to Franklin. It's a good thing we got to sleep plenty on the train because we won't be gettin' any tonight."

Oh, what words of truth came out of my mouth at that moment!

A Nashville lady walking by told us where to find the road to Franklin, and by dark Jem and I were walking along it. Yankee troops were on it, too, some on horseback, some marching. When we heard them coming, we'd go down into the rainwater ditches alongside the road or crawl under any bushes we could find. Once during the night we had to sit in ditchwater for a long spell while what seemed like an army of Yankees went marching past us fast as they could. Then we crawled up onto the road and were on our way again.

The next morning the weather was mighty strange. Although it had been rainy and windy the day before, now it was like autumn all over again, with sunshine and a strange smokiness in the sky.

Jem and I walked into Franklin, expecting to see gray uniforms, but all we saw were blue ones. We went to the Harpeth River and found an old man standing beside one end of the railroad bridge. When I asked him where the Confederate soldiers were, he said, "South of here—about five miles away. Our boys are a couple miles below here, settin' up long wooden breastworks to keep the Rebels out of town. You lads keep away from there if you know what's good for you. There's goin' to be a battle today, or I miss my guess."

When he turned away to walk north, Jem and I headed south to the Yankee breastworks. The camp there swarmed with bluebellies. Most of them were walking around or lying on the ground near their tents smoking pipes or else writing letters on paper held on their knees.

Other boys our ages were wandering about the camp being nosy, too, so nobody pestered Jem or me. I thought the Yankees looked sleepy and tired and worried, and that made me glad.

In the middle of the afternoon, a soldier mounted on a sorrel came riding into the camp, dismounted, and went into a big tent. Right after that, a bearded Yankee officer came out and said something to a boy soldier standing by with a bugle. The boy blew the bugle, and all the Yankees stopped what they were doing, buttoned up their coats, and got hold of their muskets. Officers began to run among them yelling orders. When Jem and I tried to follow them, a soldier grabbed us. He said, "You kids shouldn't be here at all. It's too late for you to run on home. Get up a tree and pray to God a Secesh cannonball don't take your heads off at the shoulders!"

A tree? I started getting scared. The scrap must be coming up fast now.

There were big sycamores growing beside the river, so Jem and I went over to one and climbed it. We went way up high near the top, where we sat on a limb to watch what would happen. We faced south to catch a sight of our boys in gray. Just thinking that they were so close made my heart swell up.

It turned out that we had a truly good view of everything that went on—a *terrible* good view, in fact. First Jem and I saw a long line of gray come out of some dark woods a distance away. The sun glittered on the musket barrels and made the colors of our Confederate stars and bars shine a bright red, blue, and white. We had brass bands and bugles, too, and drummer boys making brave noises that made you want to shout. On and on our soldiers came. I sat with my heart in my mouth now, waiting, waiting. Then all at once it came, the famous Rebel cry. Davey had once yelled it so Jem and I could hear how it sounded.

"Eee-ee-ee-ee-ee!"

I opened my throat as wide as it would go and yelled it, too. So did Jem.

Then hundreds and hundreds of Confederate soldiers shouted, "Hurrah, boys, *hurrah!"* As our men kept on coming and climbing over the breastworks, we heard the shooting of muskets. Before long we saw hand-to-hand fighting below us. Gray and blue, the armies reared up against each other at the logs, hitting with musket butts and jabbing with the knives attached to the ends of them. Officers raced around on horseback, and knots of blue and gray coats mingled together like threads in a piece of weaving. I saw blood suddenly spurting. Men grabbed at their chests and stomachs and sank down. Horses shot dead fell on top of wounded men, crushing them. I could scarce believe what I was seeing. Was this what a "scrap" was like—the howling and cursing and yelling, the bullets whining like angry bees, the thud of wood on wood, and the great thundering noises of the cannons?

At one point the fighting came so close to us that Jem and I had to climb even higher in our tree, though the branches got smaller.

A young soldier in blue came running to the foot of our tree, yelling every step of the way, he was so scared. An older man in gray came hotfooting after him with a musket. The bluebelly jumped for the lowest limb of our sycamore and started to climb it. The Confederate tried to jab him with the knife at the end of his musket, but before he could, the Yankee climbed out of reach. He came up fast toward Jem and me, and as he did, we went up higher ourselves.

When we got almost to the very top, we held tight to the trunk of the tree and looked down. The Yankee sat on the limb we'd just been on. The Confederate had his musket trained on him—and on us, too. Oh, Lord! Oh, Lord! I closed my eyes, listening for the sound of the shot that might kill me or Jem.

"Crack!" I heard it. Then I heard a cry from below us. Opening my eyes, I saw the Yankee fall head over heels down to the ground, dead.

The Confederate was still there, though. He looked down at the man he'd killed, then up at us. Then he began to reload his musket. I tried to call down to him that we were Confederates, but he couldn't hear my voice over all the noises of the battle. We waited, Jem and I, not saying a word more while he finished reloading. He lifted his musket to his shoulder and took aim; then suddenly he grinned and lowered it. Then he ran off in the direction of the fighting.

Jem told me, "He don't want to shoot no kids, Hannalee!"

"That's the truth, not even Yankee ones, which is what he must think we are."

Jem and I climbed back down again to the first branch we'd sat on and kept watching the fighting. I reckoned it was like looking into hell, and I felt sick inside. I was glad when all at once we weren't able to see any of the battleground at all. The stinking smoke from the gunpowder and the cannons covered up everything below. It stung our eyes and choked us, and there wasn't one breath of wind to blow it away.

Even though we couldn't see, we could still hear the terrible noises all around us. When it came on to darkness, we saw the red flames from the mouths of the muzzleloader cannons and the sheets of light along the ground as a whole line of soldiers shot off their muskets at once.

During one lull in the fighting, Jem said, "This is awful bad! Davey didn't tell us it was so bad as this. I don't never want to go to war. I didn't think it'd be like this."

"Neither did I. How can soldiers fight one battle after another when they're all this horrible? I bet it was this way for Pap and Davey lots of times. No wonder they didn't talk about it to us."

"What'll we do, Hannalee?"

"Stay up here till it gets quiet down there. Pray that the Confederacy wins."

So we sat in that old tree for hours and hours, waiting Twelve more times we heard our Rebel yell that meant the fighting was still going on below us.

It got cold, and our bodies were cramped from sitting so long. But we didn't dare move till the sounds of marching feet and galloping horses, loud cannons and shouting men came to an end.

Chapter Nine

Gettin' Closer

WE STAYED PUT EVEN WHEN THE NOISES HAD DIED down, because I'd made up my mind to wait till we could truly see before moving. At last a wind came up in the middle of the night, and the smoke was blown away. Jem and I saw lights below our tree. They were torches.

Once we got down out of the sycamore, we could see that there were heaps of bluecoat soldiers lying on the ground all around the breastworks. Most all of them were dead, I was sure. On the south side of the logs were piles of men in gray coats and butternut-brown jackets. They were lying there where they died, on top of each other in layers six and seven deep.

The battle of Franklin was finally over. The Yankees had pulled back in the night to the north, and the Confederates had gone back south.

My brother and I walked slowly toward the logs past dead Yankees, then up over the breastworks to get to the southern side. Pairs of Confederates who were still alive were walking around on the field with torches, like the Yankees were doing on the other side of the logs. They looked over the men on the ground, putting a torch near a fallen soldier and turning him over to see if he was still alive.

I felt like my innards had turned to icy coldness, and there was aching pain in my chest. I'd never seen dead men up so close as this, and they and the blood on them scared me. I walked as far away as I could from each body I passed.

Jem and I went up to two Confederates not far away from the logs. One of them was an old man with a short, gray-and-brown beard and an ugly squinting look in his eyes. The other was yellow-headed and not much older than I was. They'd just turned over a soldier, and both rose up as we came near. I took one look at the dead man and looked away. His face didn't seem to be there—all I could see was blood.

I wanted to scream and run, but I didn't. I took a deep breath and asked the soldiers, "Please, who won the battle here?"

The young one told me, "I'd say the cussed bluebellies did, even if they withdrew over the other side of the breastworks. South of here is all Confederate-held now. Our old Gen'ral Hood'll attack 'em in Nashville later on. He'll track 'em there and whip 'em. He's goin' to make 'em bawl for what they done to us at Franklin on the last day of November, 1864." He scratched his ear, then waggled the lower part of it, frowning.

The older one growled at us, "Where in hell did you two Yankee brats sprout from? Get out of here. This ain't no place for kids."

"No, sir, we ain't Yankees. We're the Reeds from Roswell, Georgia. We're mill hands sent north by the Yankees."

The young soldier turned to the other one to say, "I heard tell that Gen'ral Sherman done that to mill workers, Bushrod."

I said, "Our big brother's in the Roswell Guards. That's the Seventh Georgia Infantry of the Confederate Army. He's up in Virginia now. Pap was in that outfit, too."

The soldier named Bushrod snorted and said, "All right, so you ain't Yankees. You do sound like Georgia in your manner of talkin'. What are you boys doin' in these parts?"

"We're on our way home to Georgia. We want to pass through your army now."

The young soldier made us a deep bow and said, "Be so good as to pass directly on. Skedaddle as fast as you can and let us get on with what we're doin'. We have to fetch our wounded to the doctors. You go that way." He pointed and added, "Just hope nobody shoots you 'cause you ain't got the password. I can't give it to you 'cause we're not permitted."

I thanked them and we started off, when Bushrod

called us back. "Did you say the Seventh Georgia, boy?"

"Yes, sir, I did."

His face was red in the torchlight as he shook his head. He told us, "Dammit, I do believe that's the very regiment that got mauled so bad in September at Winchester, Virginia."

Jem asked, "Mauled?"

"Butchered. Men and boys by the hunderds were killed dead by the Yankees. It was even worse there than it is here, and we had five of our gen'rals killed today at Franklin and another bad wounded. You Georgians took a fearful pestling at Winchester. You'd best think of your brother as a dead man."

Dead? Davey dead? Tears sprang to my eyes. I grabbed Jem by the hand, and he and I ran—ran as fast as we could from Bushrod and the other soldier. We didn't run far, though. Once we were out of the light of the torches, we found it hard to see. We fell over something big in our way, a dead mule. One touch of its hide with my hand made me come away sticky with its blood.

Through my weeping I told Jem, "We'll stay here the rest of the night. In the morning our soldiers'll see us good enough to know we're not Yankees and'll let us pass through."

"Oh, Hannalee, what'll we do after that?"

"Same as we planned from the first. Go on home. That's what Davey would say for us to do—go home and be with Mama. She'll need us more'n ever now."

"Davey! Davey!" wailed Jem, clinging to me and rocking to and fro like the woman had done whose husband had been killed by Quantrill's men.

We didn't have any trouble going through the Confederate camp the morning of December 1. The sentries questioned us, and I answered them. Then some officers began talking to us and fed us chicory coffee and corn parched in a pan. When we were done eating, a long-shanked Texan led us to the road we had to take. He was ragged and shaggy-headed, but kindly. He said, "You shouldn't be goin' by the tent where the doctors tend to the wounded. It ain't fittin' for young 'uns to look at. I brought you another way. You jest be on your way now. I hear you're bound for home."

"Yes, sir. Do you think we'll whip the Yankees at Nashville?"

He had a quick, twisting smile. He spoke from the middle of his tobacco-stained beard. "It'd be mighty pleasant to do that. General Hood'll do his best, you can count on that. The Yankees think the war's well-nigh over, but Hood don't think so by a long shot. He'll go on tryin', even when we ain't got any more food, or bullets, either."

Jem told him, "I wish I could get a sight of Gen'ral Hood and Gen'ral Robert E. Lee, too."

This made the Texan laugh. He clapped Jem on the

shoulder and said, "I only saw old Hood one time myself, and that was from a goodly distance." Then, wishing us luck, he swung about and went toward a little campfire where four soldiers squatted, cooking corn-bread dough wrapped over their muskets' ramrods.

Jem and I walked in the direction the Texan had pointed. As we went along, we talked about home and Vickerys' Creek. It was almost as if we agreed to talk only about good kinds of things to keep our spirits up.

After going some miles, we stopped near some tall, straggly berry bushes to rest. As we sat there, we heard some strange rumbling noises. At first we thought it might be thunder because the sky had turned to gray, but there wasn't any lightning. I put my ear to the ground and listened. Sure enough, it was stomping, and somewhere not far off. Finally we heard a soft, whinnying sound. A horse!

Jem and I parted the bushes and squeezed through to a little open area. A big white horse, all saddled and bridled, was there stomping and snorting. His reins were caught in some tangled roots. We went slowly up to him. He saw us and rolled his eyes, then stood quiet, letting us come closer. The brand on his flank was CSA, Confederate States of America. He was a cavalry horse, or an officer's. He must have lost his rider during yesterday's battle and run off in the night. He was a fine-looking horse, handsome enough to be a general's mount.

Jem sucked in his breath and said, "And I thought he was thunder. He's only a horse."

I told my brother, "So did I. Thunder, that's what we'll call him. We got to get him out of here. He'll starve to death if we don't."

While Jem untangled his reins, I patted the horse's soft neck and talked to him. Then we led him out of the thicket onto the road.

An idea came to me, and I told Jem, "Mebbe we can ride him some of the way back home. You and me together probably don't weigh much more'n any gen'ral." So Jem and I mounted Thunder, and, with me handling his reins, we started south once more.

We rode a fair distance without seeing anybody before we spied a town ahead of us. When I saw it, I slid down off Thunder and told Jem, "You ride him into them trees over yonder and keep both of you out of sight till I come back."

Jem asked, "Why're you goin' to the town?"

"I want to send a letter to Rosellen. Once we get to Georgia, I won't be able to send one north, but mebbe she'll get it if I write from here."

"Are you goin' to tell her about Davey?"

"That's right."

I never did find out the name of that town. I went into the post office, which was also a general store, and bought us a sack of biscuits for our journey and a sheet of foolscap and an envelope. Standing at the store counter, I wrote:

Dear Rosellen:

I found out that Davey was killed ded in a Virginny batle in September. Remember him kindly. He luvved you good.

Hannibal Sanders

Then I folded it up, put it in the envelope, put some sealing wax the postmaster gave me on the back, and gave him five cents to send it to Indiana. He said he thought it might get to Miz Burton's house in spite of the state being all tore up now because of the fighting.

My duty done by Rosellen, I went back to Jem and mounted Thunder once more, heading him south. I told Jem, "Rosellen's free to do whatever she wants to now. I had to tell her what that Bushrod told us. Mebbe she won't never come back home now." I sighed and added, "I wonder if mebbe Davey had a suspicion that he was gonna get killed, and that was why he wouldn't marry her last summer."

Jem's arms tightened around my middle as he leaned his head against my back. He said, "Mama must feel real bad if she knows that Davey's gone, too, 'specially with her not knowin' where you and me are."

To cheer him up I said, "Well, it ain't as if she don't

have two pieces of good news on the way to her. Just think, we left Roswell on horseback, and, if our luck holds, we'll come ridin' back there the same way."

I don't know how many miles we rode Thunder that day. Nobody bothered us, though sometimes folks stared at the horse and then at us as we passed by. On the afternoon of our third day with Thunder, though, we ran into trouble. While we were trotting along through a pine forest, Thunder suddenly began to nicker. A minute later, five gray-coated riders appeared on the road in front of us. They were Confederate cavalry.

One of the soldiers yelled at us, "Pull up on that horse! Put your hands up in the air!"

As Jem and I did what they wanted, the troopers rode slowly up to us, their long-barreled pistols pointed straight at our chests.

The same man who had yelled before now called out, "Where did you get that horse?"

I knew what he meant and shouted back, "We didn't steal him! We found him. We think he run off in the battle at Franklin. We think he's a officer's horse."

"He sure is," said another cavalryman, who rode up closer to us. "Our cavalry. He's got *CSA* on him. Where were you two sprats headed on him?"

"Home to Georgia. To Roswell."

"Roswell, Georgia?" Another trooper pushed back his

felt slouch hat. He looked surprised. "What're you doin' up here in Tennessee? You ain't old enough to be in any army unless you're runaway drummer boys."

I told him, "We ain't. We're two of the mill hands the bluebellies brought up here from Georgia. We run off, and we're on our way home. If you need this horse more'n we do, we'll give him to you. We can walk. We've walked before."

"You can put your hands down now, and you'd best get off that horse. Sorry, but we got to take him with us. He's a army mount."

After Jem and I got down, I patted Thunder's neck and gave his reins to one of the soldiers. The leader tipped his hat to us. Then, with Thunder trotting along after them, the soldiers rode back into the pines. Jem and me were left standing in the middle of the road in the mud.

He said, "Well, at least they were our men. They could'a been bluebelly cavalry instead, and bluebellies would'a took Thunder away from us, too."

"They surely would'a, Jem, and they might have made a heap of trouble for us, too. We had Thunder for a while, and he took us a fair piece on the road home. If we had to lose him, it turned out to be the best way for him and for us, I reckon. Now we might as well start walkin'."

Having to walk again sure made the going slow and tiring. I didn't blame Jem one bit when, some hours later, he asked, "Could we mebbe find us another railroad to ride on?"

"No. I been thinkin' on that, too. We've passed railroad tracks south of Franklin, and I reckon there'll be more 'fore we come to Georgia. But tracks don't do anybody any good when there ain't no trains runnin' on 'em. We seen tracks but nary an engine or cars. We ain't even so much as heard a train whistle since we left Franklin. I bet you the trains goin' north to Nashville have quit runnin'. We're just goin' to have to keep walkin'."

I sniffed the air. It was cold and sharp, smelling of pine trees. There wasn't a sound to be heard, not even birds cawing. It seemed that the whole country was waiting— waiting on the war and who'd be the masters of Tennessee. I prayed it'd be our side.

That night we slept shivering under some pines. Our food was almost gone, but we'd had some luck just before sunset. We'd spied some apple trees in a clearing near a burned-down cabin. The apples were drying up on the tree and wormy, but parts of them could still be eaten. Even better, there were hickory nuts on one of the other trees, and a pocketful of them could keep a body walking for quite a spell.

We were lucky again the next morning. We passed through a little town real early, before anything but the roosters and the dogs were up. Just outside it, we caught up with a closed-top, slow-moving wagon hung all over with blue-speckle pans, black iron skillets, and copper-bottom pots. Right off, I knew it was a peddler's wagon. Peddlers used to come to Roswell now and then selling all sorts of things folks needed or took a fancy to—coffeepots and grinders, skillets, snakeroot oil, liver-complaint medicines, ribbons and laces, nutmeg and hair combs.

I told Jem, "Let's go talk with the peddler. Mama used to say that they're full of news. If he's for the South, we're Confederates. If he's for the North, we can say our pap died in the Yankee army."

"I'll remember, Hannalee."

"You remember, too, that I'm Hannibal."

Oh, but I'd be grateful for the day I could go back to being Hannalee. I wasn't all that taken with britches anymore. I'd thought it'd be better to be a boy than a girl when I was little, but now I'd changed my mind. Back in 1861 I'd even wished I'd been a man so I could go off to war, too—but not after what I'd seen at Franklin!

The peddler was an old man with white-and-gray whiskers and bushy gray hair sticking out from under his black top hat. He had red-rimmed, watery blue eyes and a red nose. He wore a gray frock coat, a white shirt with no collar or cravat, black-and-white-checkered pants, and black gaiter shoes. He looked like a lot of peddlers I'd seen.

When I called out to him, "Hey, mister," he pulled up his chestnut mare and asked in a husky voice, "Where'd you colts sprout from?"

I pointed to the town over my shoulder. "We just come through there. Where are you bound?"

"Nowhere in particular."

"You headin' south and east, mebbe?"

"Mebbe so; is that where you're headed?"

As he talked, I found myself taking to him. He talked more like a Southerner than a Yankee. I asked, "Could we go along with you for a while, since you're headin' in our direction? We'd sort of keep you comp'ny. We ain't beggin'. We got some money to pay for our food, and our pockets are full of nuts."

"Nuts, huh? I'm mighty partial to nuts. All right, you can go along with me, I reckon. I like comp'ny. Me and Callie, my mare, just mosey along. We don't move fast. Are you in a big hurry?"

I said, "Well, not in a lot of one."

If he moseyed too slow, Jem and I would leave him. I planned to get home for Christmastime, even if Jem and me had to walk day and night.

The peddler asked, "Can you make a fire and cook?"

I said, "I can cook a little. Our ma thought everybody ought to know how to boil a egg or fry up sowbelly, even boys."

He nodded. "That's commendable of her to teach her sons to do useful chores. Can you make good cush?"

"Yes, sir. I can fry up meal and water in bacon grease good as anybody else. Were you in the army, sir?"

This made him chuckle. He said, "I volunteered in 1861, but Lucius Carewe was too old for General Robert E. Lee's liking, so I went on bein' what I am—a peddler."

So he leaned to being a Confederate, too. I said, "We're the Reeds. I'm Hannibal and he's Jem."

Mr. Carewe said, "You sound to me like Georgia boys. I know Georgia voices."

I lied. "We lived in Georgia when we was little. We lived around Roswell then."

"I heard of it, but I never went there. A mill town, ain't it?"

"Yes, sir. We heard tell Gen'ral Sherman burned down the mill and took away hunderds and hunderds of mill hands to the North. Wasn't that a wicked thing to do?" I wanted to find out what he'd say to that. I wasn't so trusting as I used to be.

Carewe nodded. "It was, indeed, a terrible thing to do, but there's not much about war that ain't terrible. Was your papa ever a mill hand?"

"Yes, he was, before camp fever killed him. He was a Confederate soldier like our brother Davey, who got killed at Winchester in Virginia a couple months back."

"You lost 'em both, huh?" For a moment Mr. Carewe was silent, then he said, "Unless you want to walk, I might be able to take the two of you up beside me on the seat. You appear to have skinny rumps, so you won't crowd me. Callie won't be put out too much by pullin' you, too. Come on up here and crack some nuts for me. There's a nutcracker hangin' on the other side of my wagon."

So we traveled with Mr. Carewe for a while, going from town to town, and visiting cabins and farmhouses along the way. At night we either made a fire and cooked a supper out of doors or, if we got lucky, were asked to stay over with farm folks. It didn't take me long to notice that the places we stopped at were always owned by folks who were for the Confederacy. We heard them cuss out Abe Lincoln and every Yankee general they'd heard of. Mr. Carewe always told them we were the Reed boys from Nashville, which is what I'd told him when we began to travel with him. I wished he'd go faster so we'd get home sooner, but it was his wagon and his horse, and he wasn't asking us to pay him to go with him. It cankered me to go so slow, but riding was better than walking, and I did take to being with my own kind of folks again.

One morning, though, as we were riding beside Mr. Carewe in his wagon, he gave us a big surprise by turning to Jem and me and saying, "The woman at the house last night told me something about each of you after you both went up to her loft to sleep. Jem, she said that you're a mill hand."

Jem gasped out, "How'd she know that?"

"By the scars on your wrists. She used to work in a cloth mill here in Tennessee and said that yours were either from a cardin' machine or from your tryin' to hug a wildcat." Carewe laughed.

Jem didn't say a word. He only put his hands into his jacket pockets.

I said, "That woman was mighty nosy."

"Or just mighty observant," replied the peddler.

"Well, what'd she have to say about me?" I snapped, recalling now how the redheaded woman peered at me several times the night before.

Carewe said, "She thinks you're a mite too pretty for a boy and wonders if you'll ever need a razor."

I flared up. "Us Reeds have Cherokee blood! Indians don't ever grow a lot of hair on their faces."

"Mebbe so, mebbe so."

The peddler didn't say anything more about it, and I was so beflustered by what he'd said that I didn't say another word to Mr. Lucius Carewe all that day. How dare he pry into us Reeds' personal matters! He sure kept quiet enough about himself.

There wasn't much chance to brood on what the peddler told us, though, because that night, just after supper, two Yankee horse soldiers who saw our fire came riding into our camp. Old Mr. Carewe spotted them first and came hurrying around to the other side of the wagon to tell us. "It's Yankee cavalry. Get up into the wagon and hide. They mebbe seen me before and know I travel alone. They'd ask about you two. Let me talk with 'em."

Jem and me had no choice but to do what he said. We got up fast into the wagon and pulled Callie's night blanket over our heads. It smelled powerfully of horse, and I had to hold my nose to keep from sneezing.

Although I couldn't see them, I could hear every word the men said.

Mr. Carewe spoke first. "Good evenin'," he said really friendly-like.

Then one of the Yankees said, "I think I saw you before. In fact, I believe I bought some boot blacking from you. Where are you headed, peddler?"

"Oh, down Chattanooga way. Yep, I did sell you boot blacking, and cigars, too. But I haven't got any cigars anymore."

"Too bad," said the second Yankee. "Have you seen any Confederates hereabouts lately?"

"You mean Confederate soldiers, don't you?"

"What else would we mean, you old fool?"

Mr. Carewe didn't take offense. He still sounded friendly as he said, "I seen nary hide nor hair of anybody in a gray coat except for a louse I killed last night."

This made both troopers laugh.

Carewe asked them now, "Say, do you have any news from up around Nashville?"

"We sure do. There's been a battle there, a big one, the middle of this month. It went on for two days, but we won. Hood's army, or what's left of it, is in retreat, and we're following them. In fact, we're out scouting right now for Hood's stragglers. When our army's done, there won't be any more Confederate Army here in Tennessee or Kentucky at all. And General Sherman's sewing up Georgia right now."

"Yep, it does look like it'll be endin' soon, don't it? Well, there's nobody here with me but my old mare and some more little gray-jacket critters like the one I caught last night. You want some of 'em?"

"No, we don't need any more. We've got plenty of lice of our own. Good night to you."

A jingling noise let us know the Yankees had ridden away.

Mr. Carewe didn't call us out right off. He whistled all through "Listen to the Mocking Bird" and "Juanita" before he said, "They've skedaddled. Come on out now."

When we were down, he asked, "Did you hear what they said to me?"

"We sure did. It made for mighty poor listenin'."

"I know. I know. Well, your hearin' it saves me from tellin' you what I reckon to be true. And I also reckon that what that woman told me about you two last night is true, too. You're both mill hands, ain't you, that Sherman sent up to Indiana. You ran away and are headin' for home. And, Hannibal, you ain't no boy at all, are you? I didn't pry into your bus'ness before, but now that we're goin' to be travelin' to Georgia together, I think you should tell me the truth."

I waited a minute, then said, "Yes, sir, you're right. I'm

Hannalee. And we did run off. All we want is to get home to Roswell, Georgia." Then I stopped, not realizing till just now the rest of what he said. "You're goin' to take us all the way to *Georgia*?"

He laughed and said, "That's right. It truly appears to me that the South won't win this war. The army here in Tennessee's been whipped. That leaves only the one in Virginia. If the Yankee army that won here in Tennessee marches to Virginia in the springtime to join the Yankees there, the whole thing could be over soon. The Confederates have been holdin' Richmond, but how long can they hold out against so many Yankees? I got me a female cousin down in Atlanta, and with what I hear about Sherman's doin's down there, I think I'll go see how she's farin'. Mebbe Lily needs some help. It'd only be right for me to go look in on her."

I cried, "*Atlanta*? That's only twenty miles from home!" I flung my arms around his neck and hugged him hard as I could. Jem and me'd be home for Christmas without a doubt.

We didn't see any more Yankee patrols because Mr. Carewe took back roads all the way. One morning not long after breakfast, he stood up in the slow-moving wagon, shaded his eyes with one hand, and said, "It's hazy and foggy, but if you peer hard, you'll see old Signal Mountain. You know what that means, don't you?"

Jem answered him, "That we're close to Georgia!"

Carewe saw that I didn't look up as Jem had done and said, "You sound happy, Jem, but you ain't crowin', Missy Hannalee."

I told him, "I'm joyful, but things bother me, too."

"What kind of things?"

"Well, knowin' that home is gettin' closer and closer every day has made me do some hard thinkin'. How'll we hide in Roswell if we got to, and what'll we say to Mama about Davey? Mr. Carewe, mebbe she ain't even heard that he's dead!"

"That could be so. Then don't you tell her what you heard, either one of you."

"Not tell her?"

"No, it's the duty of the Confederacy to let her know. How'd you find out about your pa dyin'?"

"Mama got a letter from an officer in Pap's unit. But he died in a army camp, not in a battle. Don't it sometimes happen that nobody can tell who those soldiers are?" An ugly memory of the battle of Franklin raced through my head.

"That *can* happen, but it's not often. My advice is to keep what you heard to yourselves till she gets word from somebody up in Virginia. She just birthed a new baby, didn't she? Don't make her grieve no sooner than she has to and take her strength down. She'll need it to care for the baby. And don't take her joy from her at seein' the two of you again with bad news about your big brother."

I pondered what he'd said and decided he was right. I said, "Yes, we won't tell her. It'll be hard to pretend that Davey's alive, but we'll do that."

Carewe asked, "Would he be writin' to her?"

"No, he can't write. Mebbe I could write to Virginia myself and ask about his dyin'."

"You might do that later on."

That day we crossed over into Georgia. Though we rejoiced, Jem and I didn't see us go over because we had to stay hid in the back of the wagon now. There were Yankee horse soldiers around now and then, and we were afraid that if they found out Jem and I were runaway mill workers, they'd send all three of us to a Yankee jail.

The Yankees who stopped us always asked Mr. Carewe the same question: "Have you seen any Rebel soldiers around?" And he'd always answer, "Not hair nor hide of any."

Although Jem and I couldn't see the countryside going by during the day, we knew that every step Callie took brought us closer to home. The thought made fever in my blood. Finally, after two more days of traveling, Mr. Carewe went through Marietta, where we'd been kept prisoner in the cadets' school. Even though it was dusk, we could see that it was just rubble now, and mostly burned down. When we were past the town, he reined

Callie in and told us, "You have to get on out now. This is as far as I go. I've got to go on to Atlanta from here. You sprouts take the road that goes north and east of here. Do you think you can make your way home now?"

We came out of the wagon, and as we passed Mr. Carewe in the front seat, Jem and I grabbed and kissed him. I told him, "We won't never forget the name of Lucius Carewe so long as we live!"

He smiled at us and said, "I liked knowin' the pair of you jim-dandies, and I thank you for keepin' me comp'ny for a time. Merry Christmas to you, and God bless you." He tipped his hat to us and then took Callie off down the Atlanta road.

As we started off on the road the peddler pointed out, I told Jem, "It's thirteen miles to home. Do you think we can make it by daylight tomorrow, the mornin' after Christmas?"

"We can sure try."

Chapter Ten

The Persimmon-Seed Button!

THAT WAS THE SWEETEST WALK I EVER TOOK IN MY whole life. It was cold as blazes, and it rained and sleeted the whole time, but I didn't mind. I just put one foot in front of the other, keeping my mind on home. "Turn homeward," Mama had asked me. I'd said I would, and Hannalee Reed always kept her promises.

I didn't know what hour of the night it was when we got to Roswell. It was dark as the inside of a cave, but we could still see the foundations of the houses that had been burned down. The empty places made me feel sad. We crossed the town square where we'd sat for five days in the hot sun last summer, and walked to the house where Rosellen's Aunt Marilla had lived.

Jem asked, "Will we go straight up to the door, Hannalee?"

I thought for a while, then said, "No, we better not. We don't even know for sure if old Marilla still lives here. There's no tellin' what's goin' on in Roswell now that the Yankees were here. We'd better wait till morning."

"Then what'll we do?"

"Sit on the stoop and wait till daylight. We'll keep hushed up so nobody'll hear us and come out and ask why we're here. If any Yankees come along, let me do all the talkin', Jem."

So Jem and I sat on the stoop in front of Marilla Sanders's house till we saw the pale, wet sun come up over some treetops. Then, suddenly, we heard a baby crying. Yes, there was a baby in the house. In my heart I knew who that was. And if he was there, I hoped and prayed Mama was there, too.

I stood up and told Jem, "Mama's bound to be up if the baby's up. So let's go."

Jem said, "Hannalee, I'm scared. What if Mama and Marilla Sanders ain't here anymore?"

I hit Jem's arm. "Hush! Don't you think I'm scared, too? Now, you act brave even if you don't feel it."

I reached into my pocket and pulled out the persimmon-seed button. Then I went to the door with it in my hand and knocked softly.

Old Marilla Sanders, her white hair hanging down behind her in one long braid, opened the door. She did not look happy to see callers so early in the morning. No, she didn't know Jem and me by sight, and her wrinkled face was cross.

"What do you kids want?"

I asked her, "Does the Widow Reed live here?"

"Yes, she does. Who wants to know about her?"

"Me!"

Oh, how my heart jumped in me. *Mama was here!*

Now I handed the old woman the persimmon-seed button and said, "Miz Sanders, I'd thank you kindly if you'd give this to the Widow Reed. Tell her that her girl has brung somethin' home to her again that she gave her last summer."

As Marilla peered at me, her whole face changed. She cried out, *"Hannalee? Is that you? You've come home."* Then she looked past me and cried again, "Ain't that little Jem behind you?"

"Yes, ma'am, it is—we both come home."

"You sure did! You get inside here right now!" Her old, skinny hand caught hold of me by the shoulder and jerked me in. Jem followed. She said, "The Yankees have left a garrison here. Not many soldiers, but too many for me. Your ma's had her baby."

Jem asked, "Baby Paul?"

"No, Paulina. She's a girl." Marilla went on excitedly, "She's red-haired like your pa, his spittin' image. She's a Reed. You wait down here, you two. I'll go up and tell your mama you've come home. God alive, how did you ever get here? It beats all believin'."

We listened to the old woman going upstairs and opening a door. Then there came a crying, *"Hannalee! Jem! Hannalee! Jem!"*

At the sound of Mama's voice, we came thundering up

and threw ourselves onto the bed. Mama grabbed tight hold of us, while our baby sister wailed in her cradle next to the bed.

"Oh, my God. Thank you, Lord," was all Mama could say, over and over again. Finally she asked, "Where you been?"

"I been in Indiana and Jem was in Kentucky."

"How'd you get loose from the Yankees? Did they let you go?"

Jem told her, "No. We run away from 'em! Hannalee come to get me, and then we run away home together."

"Oh, my children!" Mama said softly, then she motioned toward the cradle. "There's your little sister, Paulina. Now if only Davey was here instead of in Virginia, my joyfulness would be complete. Won't it be fine when we're all together again?"

Davey? I felt a cold come quick up my back. Mama *didn't* know! Raising my eyes from Mama's happy face, I looked at Jem and found his eyes on me. Neither of us answered her.

Just then baby Paulina began crying louder. I reached down to the cradle, carefully picked Paulina up, and laid her in Mama's arms. Right off, my baby sister stopped her caterwauling and smiled at me like she knew me.

Mama told us, "She's a good baby. Now, you two lay here beside me and tell me how you got home." She opened her hand to show me the persimmon-seed button

Marilla had given her. Smiling, Mama went on, "I reckoned I'd see this again someday—that my pretty older daughter would be bringin' it home to me."

At this I took off my boy's cap, and she gasped at the sight of my cut-off hair. "Oh, Hannalee, where are your braids?"

I told her proudly, "I cut my braids off and finally left 'em up in Kentucky under a bramble bush."

Jem continued, "And I put 'em on in Tennessee and wore 'em for a spell in Kentucky."

While Mama stared at us puzzled, Jem looked over at me, and we both began to laugh. We knew that Mama would laugh, too, once we told her all about it.

When we came downstairs again to let Mama get dressed, we found Marilla Sanders getting breakfast. She straightened up from bending over the stove and asked us, "Where's Rosellen? Why didn't she come home, too?"

I'd been expecting this question, so had my answer ready. I told the old woman, "She's up in Indiana. I reckon mebbe she'll be along later on."

"What's she doin' there?"

"Workin' in a Yankee mill. She had to, or else they'd put her in jail." I had decided a while ago that I wouldn't tell her about Rosellen's prettifying herself or about Mr. Francis Greenwood or about refusing to come home with me. Instead I told another lie. "Rosellen reckoned she couldn't pass for a man or boy the way I could to get through Yankee towns and mebbe whole armies of soldiers. So we decided it would be better if only I up and left and went over the Ohio River to get hold of Jem."

"Do tell! Do tell!" Marilla shook her head. "It's a prime wonder to me you ever got back here at all!" I'd never heard her give out so much praising before to anybody. She continued, "Then Rosellen'll come back home after the war is over and marry up with your brother Davey?"

This made me look at Jem again, but he had his eyes on his grits.

I was glad that Mama picked this moment to show up. I didn't want to tell them that I didn't think either Rosellen or Davey would ever be coming home again. I changed the subject fast as I could by asking Mama, "What'll we do now that we're here? If there are still Yankees about, do you think we'll have to hide out?"

She told us, "I pondered on that while I was gettin' dressed upstairs. You two are the only mill hands who've come back here so far that I know about. There are Yankee soldiers around to keep order, they say, but I don't think it'd enter their heads that any mill hands would come back 'fore the war's ended. They won't be lookin' around for any, so I don't think we need to hide you. We'll ask the folks who know you two by sight not to let on that you were among the mill workers took away last summer. They'll be glad to do that for us. Hannalee, you might as well stay a boy for now."

I asked, "Have the Yankees started up any mills? Can we get work somewhere?"

"No, there ain't any mill work at all." Mama sighed deeply. "Marilla's a saint from heaven. The Yankees let her keep this place, and her chickens and garden are what's kept us livin' since you all went away."

Hearing this troubled me greatly. "Mama, Jem and me make two more mouths to feed. I spent almost all the money I had gettin' home to you. It's wintertime now, so there can't be anythin' left in the garden to eat. And since it's almost as cold in here as it is out of doors, I reckon you use what's left of the wood only for the kitchen stove, don't you?"

"That's true, Hannalee, we do. Some days we stay in bed under quilts because of the coldness."

"What do you eat?" asked Jem.

"Whatever we can get. We trade for some things, but mostly we eat cush when we have bacon grease, or cornmeal mush, eggs, or these grits. We don't see much sowbelly these days."

Marilla Sanders's chuckle wasn't joyful. She said, "It ain't that there's not any more hogs in Georgia. It's that the Yankee armies took 'em and everythin' else they could lay their hands on when Gen'ral Sherman came through."

I said, "Well, Jem and me don't intend to be a burden

on you. We'll work at whatever we can put our hands
on to keep us livin' till springtime. Have you got seeds
for another garden?"

"You bet I have!" said Marilla. "Last spring I didn't
sow all the seeds I had, and I saved the ones from last
summer's crop. With you and Jem here to help, we'll be
just fine once spring and summer come. And mebbe my
Rosellen girl and your brother Davey will be home in
time to help with the harvestin'."

Oh, Lordy, I could see that there was misery ahead for
Jem and me come summertime.

The next few months were hard, terrible hard. We
didn't have enough to eat, and though Jem and I went out
every day looking for work, we didn't find much. Sometimes we'd hold a Yankee's horse for him, and he'd give
us a penny or two. Then we'd be able to buy a few
supplies at the store. Sometimes we'd dig up root vegeta-
bles in a field that everyone else had overlooked, or we'd
find old dried-up yams or sweet potatoes in the root cellar
of a burned-down house. Jem and I ranged a distance from
Roswell, walking in the cold and keeping our eyes open
for whatever would fetch us money or feed us. We fished
in Vickerys' Creek, but didn't get much more than min-
nows for our trouble. We even went up to Yankee horse
soldiers and asked them to let us glean from under their
horses. Yankees carried rations of corn to feed their

mounts, and what the horses didn't get into their mouths fell to the dirt. Jem and I would pick up this feed kernel by kernel and put it all inside Jem's cap. At home Mama would parch it and grind it up for flour.

Most times while we were crawling around under the horses, the Yankees talked to each other just like we weren't there at all. That was how we got our news about the war and about what was happening in Georgia. We heard that General Sherman's four armies had torn up railroad tracks, heated them red-hot in fires, and wound them around trees so they could never be straightened out and used again. We learned that there was still Confederate cavalry riding in the state, picking off Yankee soldier stragglers, cutting their throats, and leaving them dead beside the roads as a warning to other bluebellies coming along that way. And we found out that a Yankee general named Grant had our army holed up near Richmond, Virginia, and was starving them out.

On the first of March, 1865, Aunt Marilla, Jem, and I planted a garden.

There still wasn't one word to Mama about Davey. Jem and I mourned him secretly but never said anything about what we knew. By now I doubted that Mama would ever hear—not with the war going so badly. All of Georgia was held by Yankees since Sherman had got to the sea at Savannah. Even if a letter had been sent about Davey, how could it get through to us? Someday I'd have to tell Mama the terrible bad news. I was now the oldest one, so it had to be me. But how I dreaded the idea of that hateful day.

Finally the war ended! Our head general, Robert E. Lee, surrendered to the Yankees in Virginia early in April. It grieved us all, but at the same time we hadn't held on to the idea of winning for some time now.

Jem came running home with the news from the town square, where Yankee soldiers were shooting off their muskets to celebrate.

When Mama found out, she softly said, "Paul," like she was telling Pap something. Then she said, "Davey'll be comin' home now! Our men'll be mustered out of the army."

After she'd gone up to bed, Jem whispered to me behind Marilla's turned back, "Should you go up and tell Mama about Davey now, Hannalee?"

"No, I can't. Not yet!"

"I don't blame you. Our losin' the war's bad enough news right now, huh." He went out into the backyard, then came back to me in a hurry. "There are cannons makin' the night skies red from the direction of Atlanta. I reckon it's the Yankees celebratin' there. Do you want'a see it?"

"No, I don't. I seen enough cannons in the nighttime to last me the rest of my life. Go to bed, Jem. Marilla's already gone on up."

He left me alone below, and I sat in the dark for a time

thinking of how Davey and I had stood outside together almost a year ago, looking at the cannon fire from the battle of Kennesaw Mountain.

One day right after General Lee surrendered, while Mama and I were sitting in the doorway of the house shelling spring peas for supper, we heard that President Abraham Lincoln had been shot and killed in Washington, D.C. Marilla fetched us the news from the general store. It had just come in over the telegraph.

Mama said softly, "So the Yankees are grievin', too." Tears had come into her eyes. She patted my hand and went on. "Everybody grieves in this war, don't they?"

Oh, how right Mama was. Back in 1861, when the fighting had just started, it had been so exciting to see Davey and Pap go off to war to the music of a brass band with the Roswell Guards. How proud Rosellen had looked as she walked beside Davey. He had grabbed and kissed her as the whole town cheered. But that had been all there was about the war that was joyful. How soon all that changed. How soon we all found out what a hellish bad thing it really was. If there'd never been a war, both Papa and Davey would be alive and home with us right now. While I let the tiny green peas slip from my fingers into the bowl in my lap, I prayed that Jem wouldn't ever have to go off to fight any wars when he grew up.

This was the proper time to tell Mama about Davey, but the words stuck in my throat. I strangled on what I wanted to say but couldn't get it out. Here it was coming on to late springtime, and there still wasn't any news about him. I knew what this probably meant. He'd died up at Winchester, a place I'd never even heard of before but would never forget now. He was hurt so horrible during the fighting that they'd buried him as an unknown Southern soldier.

When our Confederate soldiers started to come home, Mama naturally began to keep watch for Davey. The men came home ragged, mostly skin and bones, walking through Roswell in twos and threes. They didn't talk much. They just drifted through in their dirty gray and butternut coats, torn pants, and old hats. Sometimes they were even barefooted.

Us Reeds didn't have anything to give them in the way of food or clothes, but sometimes I'd fill a canteen of water for one, and he'd tell me he'd been in Cobb's Legion or some other Georgia outfit. But no one I talked to ever knew any Davey Reed from Roswell. Nobody came back from Davey's outfit yet. I knew some of them would be along home sooner or later, and I dreaded their coming—that's when Mama would have to learn the bad news.

The evening of June the first came, and we still had

heard nothing. The day before, Mama had told us just as we were getting ready to go to bed, "My bones tell me we'll get some news tomorrow. I think it'll be about Davey."

This had chilled my spine and made me shiver. But I still said nothing.

Jem asked, "Mama, is it your Cherokee blood tellin' you this?"

"It surely is. The Cherokee in me never fails. Didn't I just know that you and Hannalee would come home even though the Yankees took you far away?"

Mama's words hadn't comforted me, and all that first day of June I pondered them and waited for something to happen. By suppertime I reckoned she'd been wrong.

Marilla Sanders ordered us to sit down and eat. These days she was more cantankerous-natured than usual, probably because she was looking for Rosellen to come home, too. That would be some more bad news I'd have to tell sooner or later.

We were halfway through supper when we heard it— the knocking on the door. Mama cried, *"Davey! Davey's come home! Come on in, Davey!"* and rose up out of her chair.

I couldn't move. Neither did Jem. This couldn't be happening! We could only turn our heads and stare at the door as it opened slowly.

Then in he came! Thin as a bed slat, ragged all over,

and black-bearded. But he was our brother—this scarecrow was our Davey!

Mama got to him first and hugged him, then Marilla and Jem. I just busted out in tears at the fine sight of him. When Davey saw me crying, he stared at me for a minute, then began to laugh. He said, "Is that you, Hannalee, lookin' like a boy with your hair cut off?" Then he hugged me real tight.

But it was only one arm that was going around me! I pulled away and looked at him real good now. For the first time I saw that he only had one arm. His left arm was cut off just above the elbow, and his coat sleeve below that was empty.

"Davey," I cried out. "You been wounded bad! What happened? Did you get hurt at the battle of Winchester?"

"Winchester?" he said, looking puzzled. "I never was at Winchester." He gestured toward his arm and continued. "I lost this at Petersburg. The Yankee doctors cut it off when I got captured. I reckon that saved my life, 'cause my arm was bad infected from a bullet that hit me. I been in a Yankee prison hospital ever since. I wasn't at Appomattox when Gen'ral Lee had to give up to the Yankee gen'ral though some of my outfit was. I can't truly say I was sorry to miss out on that sorrowful day. Even bein' in a bluebelly hospital was better'n bein' there. Didn't you get the letter my captain wrote about my gettin' hurt? I knowed he wrote it. He said he would."

I said, "No, Davey, there never was any letter from you."

"But he wrote two to you and one to Rosellen." He sighed. "I guess they never got through. I gave 'em to soldiers who were goin' home on leave near here, but maybe they didn't make it this far south."

He looked around at all of us and asked, "Where's Rosellen?"

Mama told him, "Not here yet, Davey. A whole lot's happened since you left."

Davey nodded. "I know about the mill. I walked past it. And I heard about what Sherman did to the mill workers. I just hoped and prayed that he'd have let women and children be." He stared at the table as he talked, then he began to sniff. "What's for supper? Am I invited? First I need to eat. Then I want to talk. I ain't et since last night."

Mama flung her arms around him again. "Oh, Davey, Davey. I wish it was roasted ham fit for a king, but it's only greens and hominy."

"It don't matter. It'll be the best meal I've had since I left here last summer."

After supper we talked and talked and talked. Mama told him about his brand-new baby sister, who was lying asleep in her cradle upstairs. Then Jem and I told Davey about where we had been and all that had happened since we last saw him. And now for the first time we told what that soldier Bushrod had said about the battle of Winchester and how we thought he was dead and we were keepin' it from Mama to save her from grieving yet. When she heard this, Mama kissed both of us and started to sob.

At the end of all our talking, Davey said, "So you thought I was a dead man, huh? Well, little sister, you did do much, didn't you? You and Jem are really somethin'. You make me proud of you."

Mama got up now, took one of the two candles from the table, and told us, "All this excitement has made me a little weary." To Davey she said, "Welcome home. You say Hannalee and Jem are special. You know, I think all three of you are. My dearest ones, I think the three of you hung the moon in the sky!" Then she kissed us each on the cheek and went up to bed.

Davey had taken up pipe smoking in the army. He now asked Jem to fill a new pipe for him and light it with a sliver from the stove. Then he turned to me, looked me straight in the eyes, and said, "Now tell me about Rosellen. I took note that you pretty much left her out of your story, Hannalee."

I glanced from him to Marilla Sanders, who was knitting for Paulina and stopped as soon as she heard Rosellen's name mentioned. The time to tell this had come, I reckoned. So I sighed and began. "I don't think Rosellen'll ever come home to us, Davey. She's doin' fine at that Indiana mill she's workin' in. Besides, when I heard that you were dead, I wrote her a letter from Tennessee sayin' that you got killed in battle. I reckoned us Reeds owed tellin' her that. You could mebbe go up to Cannelton now and fetch her back home—claim her, I mean. Or I could write her another letter and say that I made a mistake and you ain't dead after all—just wounded."

Old Marilla got up now and went out onto the front porch, leaving her knitting behind. Davey just smoked for a long spell, letting the smoke drift out the open window. Finally he said, "No. You say Rosellen's doin' fine up North. What have I got to offer her? Not one cent—not even two arms. I should'a wed her when she wanted to. I thought plenty on that in Virginia. I've lost her. I missed my chance to have her. Let her think I got killed. Let her make herself a life up there in Yankee land. I reckon even if it's only been a year, I've already changed too much for her now."

"I think by now Rosellen's changed too much for you, too."

"Most likely. I'll think on her as somethin' else I lost in the war. She mebbe will think of me the same way."

"I think she might."

We sat there together, Davey smoking and me just looking at him. Finally I broke the quiet. "What'll you do now, Davey?"

"I know what I *want* to do. I know what all of us Reeds will do—move away from here to Atlanta. That city will be buildin' up again 'fore too long. Folks are comin' back home to it already. I'm a carpenter by trade. There'll be work in Atlanta for me even with one arm. One arm swings a hammer. Teeth hold nails. We'll pick up and leave here. The mill might never be rebuilt, or it could take months before they start. I got to find work *now*. So, it'll be Atlanta." Then he said, "We'd all better get some rest now. We're goin' to get started on our new life first thin' tomorrow. Where should I sleep? Will it be the bench or the floor?"

"I dunno. I'll go ask Marilla. It's her house, not ours."

I went outside and found Marilla sitting in the dark, rocking slowly back and forth in a rocking chair. I sat down on the top step beside her. "I heard what you and Davey said," she told me. "I know in my heart that Rosellen won't never come home. I reckon your mama will ask me to go to Atlanta with you. But I'm too old to move. I'll stay put here till I die." She kept rocking and went on, "Davey's only twenty-one as I reckon it, but he heads your fam'ly now. Go where he takes you, Hannalee. He'll mourn Rosellen, but he's young and mighty good to look at. He'll look at the pretty girls in Atlanta, and they'll look back at him. With his one arm, they'll think he's a hero. That one arm'll let everybody who sees him know what he did in this heart-hurtin' war."

I told her, "I hope you're right. I hope Davey and Rosellen will both be happy someday. They've changed —both of 'em."

"We all have. You and Jem come home changed, even

if you don't know it yet. Your ma's changed, and even me, old as I am. That, I reckon, is one of the worst thin's about a war—how it changes folks, changes 'em faster 'n most anythin' else in life except a truly bad sick spell. Yes, that's what the war's like, a terrible bad sickness. Give me your hand, Hannalee."

She took my hand in the darkness and said, "You've got a strong hand for a girl. Atlanta'll be needin' all kinds of strong hands. You go there, and if you be as smart as I think you are, you'll learn somethin' better than mill work. Learn your letters good. Better yourself. Be what you can be. Have you got a aim in life yet?"

"Yes, ma'am."

"What'll it be, you June bug?"

"I reckon I'd fancy bein' a teacher. I used to want to work in a mill office, but I don't want that now."

"You be a teacher, then. It's a fine aim in life. You'll fetch home a star in whatever you set your mind to. What'll I do with the one gold piece and the gold ring I been savin' for the day Davey and Rosellen wed?"

"I wish I could tell you, Aunt Marilla. It's your money and your ring. Davey wants to know where you want him to sleep—the bench or the floor?"

She chuckled. "You go tell him to put his bedroll and his sweet self wherever he wants to in my house—I'm that pleased to see him home!"

Author's Note

THE FIRST HALF OF THIS NOVEL IS FACT, THE SECOND half fiction—or, more correctly, the result of some "educated" guessing as to probable events that could have taken place in the lives of my characters after midsummer 1864.

When most people think of the American Civil War, their minds immediately conjure up Margaret Mitchell's classic novel, *Gone With the Wind*. This book not only portrays a memorable set of characters and chronicles a host of stirring events, but leaves many readers with a lasting impression of what life in the South was like during the 1860s. That picture is chiefly one of a plantation-based aristocracy with the land cultivated by black slave labor.

This is by no means the entire historical picture of the South, however. As in all societies, the Southern aristocracy represented only a tiny proportion of the population.

The bulk of nonblack Southerners were not great land-owners. They were small farmers, townsfolk, merchants, and industrial workers.

The aristocrats furnished the officers of the Southern armies. The common soldiers, on the other hand, were usually not slaveholders. In general, they were not well off; often they were "dirt poor." They fought for the Confederacy because they felt themselves to be Southern-ers.

As mill workers, my fictional Reed family of Roswell, Georgia, were not of the class who would have fit in with the characters of *Gone With the Wind*. Yet there were many like the Reeds—people whose lives were totally disrupted by the war and whose menfolk died by the thousands in the many battles fought between 1861 and 1865. Davey Reed is, I am sure, more typical of the Southern soldier than Ashley Wilkes or Rhett Butler—though not so glamorous and dashing.

I feel that young readers should be aware of the Daveys, the Hannalees, the Jems, and the Rosellens. They also have tales to tell, though theirs are not of balls, barbecues, and blooded horses, but of quiet heroism. They do not have a beautiful Tara to remember and strive to preserve, yet they have no less love for the homes they knew before the War. Soldiers who owned nary a blade of grass nonetheless thought of their homes and longed to return to them.

THE AMERICAN CIVIL WAR

The battle of Gettysburg, which took place in early July 1863, before my story begins, can be considered one of the most important of the American Civil War. At that time, Southern troops under the command of General Robert E. Lee penetrated as far north as this Pennsylvania town. After a costly defeat suffered there, they retreated south again, never to take northern roads so far again. Gettysburg is said by many historians to be the "turning point" of the War, signaling the beginning of a decline in Southern strength.

Between 1863 and 1864 the war was fought on a number of fronts. The most important were in Virginia (Richmond was the capital of the Confederate states) and in the west along the Mississippi and Ohio rivers. While General Lee was entrenched in Virginia fighting battles in the east, other Confederate forces were fighting in the west.

William Tecumseh Sherman was one of the most renowned Union (Yankee) Army generals. He operated chiefly in the west. By this time the Yankees had secured Tennessee and held Kentucky, which was neutral, in a firm grasp. In the spring of 1864 Sherman came into Georgia and fought at Resaca and later at Kennesaw Mountain. From the latter battlefield he swung around Atlanta to attack other parts of the state. His cavalry under young General Kenner Garrard rode to Marietta,

Roswell, and New Manchester, avoiding Atlanta. It was not until later that same summer that Atlanta was abandoned to Sherman by the South's very aggressive general John B. Hood, whose personality could not endure a siege. He moved his army out of the city into Alabama.

In the early autumn of 1864 Lee's forces in Virginia were battling another famous Union general, Ulysses S. Grant. Late in the year the controversial General Hood, who preferred attack to defense, decided to make a very bold, but for the South foolhardy, move. With the army he had taken out of Atlanta, he marched up through Tennessee and on November 30 met the Union forces under General John M. Schofield in battle at Franklin. Hood lost. After this defeat he marched north and attacked nearby Nashville on December 15–16. He lost there, too, and his shattered, demoralized army never attempted to take Tennessee again. His forces more or less disbanded and fled south, pursued by Yankee troops.

In the meantime, General Sherman left Atlanta and traveled down through Georgia with his army divided into four lines, each marching ten miles apart. They lived off the land and left great suffering in their wake. Marching with such a great number of men, he found little opposition from the Home Guard or from Confederate cavalry. When Sherman reached the sea, he turned and marched north toward Virginia, joining his army with General Grant's.

The South was doomed! Robert E. Lee surrendered to Grant at Appomattox, Virginia, in April 1865, and the Civil War was over.

THE ROSWELL MILL WORKERS

Every war creates "displaced persons," and the American Civil War was no exception. The saga of the Georgia textile workers is historical fact. In July 1864 Yankee cavalry sent by General Sherman under General Garrard arrived in Roswell, Marietta, and New Manchester, Georgia. The Yankee troopers burned mills in Roswell and New Manchester after the Confederate cavalry guarding these towns had withdrawn.

Because they helped the Southern cause by making cloth and roping for the Confederate Army, the mill hands were considered traitors to the Union. Garrard proceeded to round them up. In Roswell over four hundred mill workers, chiefly women and children, with a few older men sprinkled among them, were held for five days in the town square in the intense summer heat. When Sherman's officer in charge asked for instructions regarding the Roswell mill hands, Sherman replied, "Send them to Indiana and turn them loose!"

While the mill workers waited for transport wagons, whiskey stores began to appear in Roswell. Later the whiskey got into the hands of some of the Yankee guards. Drunken soldiers forced their attentions on the women mill hands, many of whom were young and pretty. At this critical moment a fortunate historical coincidence occurred. Some sober Yankee cavalrymen arrived on the scene and, on command from a quick-thinking officer, took the mill hands up behind them on their horses and conveyed them to the nearby town of Marietta. Here they were held for a time in the buildings of the deserted military school. Mill workers from other Georgia communities were also collected and brought under guard to this temporary prison.

Nearly two thousand mill workers were given rations and put on trains heading north. Some remained at Nashville, Tennessee, for a time. Others were sent on to Louisville, Kentucky. Some sympathetic newspaper accounts of the day told of their arrival.

There were also notices in the papers advertising the services of these so-called refugees. The notice I have used in this book is an actual one. These mostly illiterate women, girls, and boys were more or less parceled out to whoever needed an employee. Families were, of course, split up in the process. Some went to work in Northern textile mills. Newspaper notices of the time indicate that others probably became hired boys and girls, seamstresses, and household servants. Those who refused to work for Northern employers were jailed.

At this point the historical accounts of the Georgia mill workers come to an abrupt end. There are no more newspaper pieces and no official government records. Some eighteen hundred people simply dropped out of sight, creating a history-mystery.

A HISTORICAL MYSTERY

From the moment in my story when Rosellen Sanders crosses the Ohio River to Cannelton, where a mill did exist in 1864, this book becomes fiction, for no one knows what became of hundreds of actual mill hands who never returned. They must have suffered terrible but unchronicled anguish. There are conjectures about the possible fates of the many who did not come home, however. One theory is that many of the young women met and married Northern men. Another is that, being penniless, some turned to prostitution in Northern cities. In neither case would the women have come home, for fear of being called "collaborators." They would have been shunned by family and former friends, and would surely not have been employed in the mills where they had worked before. The mill-hand children could have melted into Northern families or, at the very least, been prevented by force from going home. Other mill workers could have died of disease on their long journey north or while working in Northern mills. Not only was mill work hard, but the air was filled with lint and fibers that gave rise to some pulmonary diseases that were incurable in the nineteenth century. Whatever the reasons, it is historical fact that many of the displaced Georgia mill workers never returned home. The town of New Manchester no longer exists. The Roswell mill, however, was reconstructed and reopened, but it was run by new workers.

In this story I have solved this mystery for three fictional mill hands. One of them, Rosellen Sanders, does not come home. She is a spirited, proud young woman whose resentment toward her sweetheart and whose appreciation of the better conditions she finds in the North cause her to stay there.

Of a different stripe, yet as much of a "survivor" as Rosellen, is Hannalee, whose promise to her mother causes her to find her brother and "turn homeward" despite the hardships such a journey would entail.

Hannalee Reed's journey home is one that could have taken place. To mark its progress, I have used Civil War—era maps. Some towns that were prominent then are no longer so, and vice versa. I have also used railroad maps from that time to plot her journey. Their routes today may be different, or superhighways may have taken their places.

It would not have been unlikely for Hannalee to have encountered the notorious William Quantrill, the ex–Confederate Army colonel turned bushwhacker–outlaw, in Kentucky in 1864. Although most historians consider him to be a Kansas-Missouri figure, and it is generally true that most of his terrible actions took place in those states, in 1864 and early 1865 he drifted in and out of Kentucky and Arkansas. In May of 1865 he came to Huntsville and to Hartford, Kentucky, to steal horses for his band. On May 10 Quantrill and some of his men were attacked by Union soldiers near Smiley, Kentucky, while sheltering from the rain in a barn. When the bushwhackers attempted to ride out, they were fired upon. Quantrill was gravely wounded and subsequently taken to a Louisville hospital. He died on June 5, 1865, some weeks after the Civil War had come to an end. Certain purported members of his gang survived him and went on to earn reputations of their own. Among them were Cole Younger and his brothers and two other brothers, Frank and Jesse James.

Hannalee's journey takes her through Tennessee in late 1864 and has her observe the battle of Franklin. The fighting began during the afternoon of November 30 and continued into the night. Though the battle went on for only six hours, it was a bloodbath and a defeat for the Confederacy. The weather that day was strange. The air was completely still, with no wind to blow away the smoke obscuring the field. (I do not draw a grateful veil over the terrible events of the day; Nature herself did that.)

I have described the wartime hardships in "occupied" Georgia as they were. General Sherman had vowed to make Georgia "howl," and he did. Georgians suffered greatly from hunger, which was brought on by Yankee confiscation of their food supplies. They not only lost personal property taken by Sherman's men, but sometimes saw their homes and towns burned before their eyes. Attacks on their persons were not unheard of. Beatings were meted out to those who resisted Yankee confiscations or disobeyed military orders. For a century and more, General Sherman's name was a hated one in Georgia.

The lack of news about loved ones in the army and the entire progress of the war in late 1864 and early 1865 created added anguish for Southern families.

Communications between different sections of the war-torn South would be most tenuous. Telegraph service could be easily disrupted. Letters to and from loved ones in the army, often carried by furloughed soldiers, sometimes never reached their destinations. The nonarrival of Davey Reed's letters would be quite in order historically. The erroneous information about his battle actions and subsequent death were also very possible. Such misinformation resulted in not a few men thought dead (among them one of my own great-grandfathers) returning home after the war to greet a "widow" who was still a wife.

It may seem odd that, in writing of Georgia during the Civil War period, I seldom mention the black populace, then such an integral part of Southern society. It is cer-

tainly not because I am unaware of their economic impor-
tance or of the injustice and miseries of slavery. It is rather
that this book is about mill workers, and there were very
few blacks working in the mills in 1864. Supposedly there
were none in the labor force at Roswell, and in nearby
New Manchester only a few. These few would have been
slaves hired out by white masters. Most Southern blacks
were tied to agriculture and would have picked the cotton
the mills processed and made into cloth—not gone into
the mills themselves. In any case, all black mill hands were
at once freed by the Union cavalrymen, since the Emanci-
pation Proclamation was in effect. Accordingly, they
would never have been among the mill hands taken from
Georgia as "traitors" to the North.

I do not know if blacks were employed as mill hands
in Cannelton, Indiana, in 1864. It is possible, but, if so,
I have no specific information to support this.

In the North and in Yankee-held states, free and freed
black men were taken into the Union Army, where some
distinguished themselves as soldiers. Blacks were not re-
cruited into the Confederate Army except as members of
labor battalions.

In the writing of *Turn Homeward, Hannalee,* I do not
claim to write the actual Southern speech of 1864–65. I
have attempted to approximate it using whatever sources
I could find, such as the short pieces of William Gilmore

Simms and Civil War diaries. Any dialect is very difficult for young readers of another section of the country to understand. So, I have tried instead to give a sense of how Hannalee Reed and her family and friends would have spoken. Having tested my conversations in this novel on some Georgians of today who were entertained by the antique expressions they had not heard for many years, I was told that I have captured the flavor of Southern dialects and written what they think would have been right for their ancestors.

The July 1982 issue of *Atlanta* magazine carried a piece by Barbara Thomas that set me thinking about writing a book on the Roswell mill hands. It is called "The Roswell Women." The sharp eyes of my Civil War "buff" mother, Jessie Robbins, of Monterey, California, led her to send me this fascinating article. For this I am most grateful to her.

In writing *Turn Homeward, Hannalee,* I owe debts of gratitude to Louise Conti of the Roswell Public Library, Roswell, Georgia, who sent me photocopied materials; Margaret Barks of the Indianapolis Public Library, Indianapolis, Indiana; Mary E. Martin, Cobb County Public Library System, Marietta, Georgia; Dr. James Parsons, Dr. Hal Bridges, and Dr. Roger Ransom, all from the University of California, Riverside; and Phyllis Draper Fraser, a California weaving enthusiast whose Massachu-

setts family are textile manufacturers. I wish also to thank the real Charlotte Burton, a former teacher of children's literature, who gave me permission to put her into this book as a character.

Patricia Beatty
June 1983

setts family are textile manufacturers. I wish also to thank the real Charlotte Burton, a former teacher of children's literature, who gave me permission to put her into this book as a character.

Patricia Beatty
June 1983